W9-AHS-492
3 1668 01346 6153

FORT
WORTH
PUBLIC
LIBRARY

FORT

LARGE PRINT FICTION DAILEY

Dailey, Janet
Six white horses /

08/02/13

six white horses

JANET DAILEY

six white horses

Thorndike Press • Thorndike, Maine

Library of Congress Cataloging in Publication Data:

Dailey, Janet.
    Six white horses.
    1. Large type books. I. Title.
    [PS3554.A29S54 1988]   813'.54 —   88-24478
    ISBN 0-89621-194-0 (alk. paper)

Copyright © 1977 by Janet Dailey.
All rights reserved.

All the characters in this book have no existence outside the imagination of the author and have no relation whatsoever to anyone bearing the same name or names. They are not even distantly inspired by any individual known or unknown to the author, and all the incidents are pure invention.

Large Print edition available by arrangement with Mills & Boon, Ltd., England.

Cover design by James B. Murray.

six white horses

CHAPTER ONE

The horse moved restlessly, his coat shimmering with blue black hues. Its midnight color was contrasted by white saddle and bridle stitched with black leather and inset with black roses. White stockings were wrapped around the horse's legs and its impatient, dancing hooves were painted a silvery gray.

An aging man stood at the black's head, neatly dressed in a Western suit of light blue that accented the youthfulness of his build. His peppered gray head was turned to the boyishly slim girl hurrying toward him.

"What kept you, gal?" he asked with sighing patience. "They're ready to start the Grand Entry."

"The zipper got stuck on my slacks," she explained quickly, and effortlessly vaulted into the saddle, taking the reins he handed her.

The white pantsuit she wore matched the leather trappings of the horse, black roses embroidered on the pant legs and the shoulders and back. Dark brown hair was caught at the nape of her neck and plaited into a single braid.

"Knock 'em dead, honey!" he called out to her as she reined the horse away.

"I will, gramps!" Her hand raised in a cheery salute as the powerful hindquarters of the horse muscled to leap into a canter.

Not until they neared the stands of the rodeo arena did Patty King slow the black horse's pace. Weaving through the congestion of horses and riders, mostly rodeo contestants, she smiled at the teasing remarks at her tardiness from those she knew. Butterflies beat their wings against the walls of her stomach as she halted the black horse behind a pair of golden palominos whose riders were carrying the flags.

The gates into the arena were closed. Already there was activity in the bucking chutes while the steady hum of the crowd in the stands indicated their impatience for the rodeo to begin. Patty laid a soothing hand on the black's neck, quieting him with a few softly spoken words.

"Hey, Princess!" a voice called out to her as a leanly built cowboy jumped from the rail and walked toward her, flamboyantly dressed in a brightly figured Western shirt with leather chaps and jangling spurs.

"Princess?" Patty laughed her surprise,

8

brown eyes dancing at the youthfully handsome face that stopped beside her.

"You're too little to be a king, so you have to be a princess," he winked. Grabbing the over-sized saddle horn of her trick saddle and sticking the toe of his boot in the stirrup, he pulled himself up to her level, balancing himself with his other hand placed on the cantle. "I need a kiss for luck, Princess."

"Jack Evans, the last time I gave you a kiss for luck, you were bucked off the first jump out of the chutes." Twin dimples appeared in her cheeks.

An expression of mock seriousness spread across the face that was so near to hers. "You couldn't have put your heart into it. We'll simply have to keep trying until you get it right."

There was a rueful shake of her dark brown head at the sheer hopelessness of arguing with this cocky cowboy. Patty King had known him too long to be taken in by his considerable charm. Not another word of protest was offered as his mouth covered hers in a light but linger-ing kiss.

"Much better," he grinned, and swung away from her onto the ground.

"If all that mushy stuff is over," a growl-ing voice said from the arena gate, "we'll get

9

this rodeo started."

A faint pink of embarrassment flowed into her cheeks as Patty glanced at the older, battered-looking cowboy at the gates, his left arm in a plaster cast.

"I'm ready, Lefty," she said.

Grumbling silently, he nodded his acknowledgment. But her brown eyes had slid past him, caught by a pair of metallic blue. Self-consciously Patty stiffened with resentment at the mocking steel gaze. It belonged to the big, burly man just mounting the top rail of the arena fence.

Tall with powerful shoulders, there was not an ounce of spare flesh on his deceptively lean frame. Curling jet black hair was visible under his hat brim. Every feature cried out with the aggressive thrust of his masculinity. Beneath thick black brows, sooty lashes outlined the brilliant blue eyes. As Patty met their gaze, she glared her dislike of their owner, Morgan Kincaid.

The arena gate was swung open and the rodeo announcer was proclaiming the start of the rodeo. The Grand Entry parade was concluded with the presentation of colors and the playing of the National Anthem.

When the rest of the horses and riders in the Grand Entry left the arena, Patty followed,

10

pulling her black horse to a stop just inside the gate. Irritation smoldered near the surface at the sight of Morgan Kincaid swinging down from the fence rail and walking toward the chutes.

He was the antithesis of what she liked in a man. He had none of the quiet courtesy that she admired. His very presence was abrasive, setting her teeth on edge as effectively as the whine of a dentist's drill. He was aggressively male with none of the rough edges smoothed to be handsome. Patty's concentration was so intent on the wide powerful shoulders that she nearly missed her cue from the rodeo announcer.

"Our special attraction for this evening, ladies and gentlemen, is Miss Patricia King," he announced, "a native of New Mexico, a truly fine trick rider and Roman rider. Patty, give them an example of what they'll see later on this evening."

Reining the black horse in a full circle to the right, its signal for the flat-out run, Patty took him into the arena. She went once around in a hippodrome stand, falling away on the second circle to a side drag that left the crowd gasping before they broke into applause.

There was no opportunity to stay and watch the first rodeo event, which was saddle bronc riding. Patty had to return to the stable area to help her grandfather harness the six white horses she used for the Roman ride. By the time the black leather trappings were on each horse and Patty had changed into a black outfit with white roses, she was due in the arena for her performance. With her grandfather Everett King walking at the head of Liberty, the left horse in the front pair, Patty sat bareback astride Loyalty, the right horse of the last pair.

The arena lights caught the sparkles dusted over the hindquarters of the six white horses as they pranced into the arena to the tune of "She'll Be Comin' Round the Mountain." Patty's stomach was twisted in knots of nervous excitement. Rising to stand on the rosined back of Loyalty, she clucked comfortingly to the horses, taking an extra wrap on the six black reins, three in each hand. Oblivious to the announcer's words, she shifted her left foot to Landmark's back, easing the horses into a slow canter while she adjusted herself to the rhythm.

Two circles of the arena eased her attack of jitters. While Patty guided the three pairs of horses into a series of figure eights that required a flying change of lead, her grandfather supervised the setting of the hurdles. There was one jump on one side of the arena and a double jump on the opposite side.

01346 6153

Deftly checking Landmark's habit of rushing the jump, the horses cleared the barrier with faultless precision, one pair following the other and with Patty balancing a foot on each back of the last two horses. The double jump was trickier on the opposite side of the arena. As the last pair of horses was landing from the first obstacle, the first pair was taking the second.

When all the horses had cleared the last jump, it was once around the arena and a sliding stop in the center where they all took a bow with Patty standing triumphantly on their backs, a hand poised in the air in acknowledgment of the applause. A refusal at any of the jumps by any of the horses would have meant a nasty fall for Patty as well as for the horses.

Wheeling the horses toward the gate, she slipped astride Loyalty's back. A beaming smile split her face as she met the silently congratulatory expression of her grandfather. With the agility of a young man, Everett King caught Liberty's halter, slowing him to a walk through the gate and forcing the rest to do the same. A cowboy grabbed Lodestar's head while another took her grandfather's place with Liberty.

"You did a grand job, Patty," he winked at her as he laid a hand on the shining neck of Loyalty.

"You did the training. You deserve the credit," she refused in a sincere and breathless voice. "Thanks, grandpa."

His gnarled and weathered hand closed over hers affectionately, before a somber look stole over his face. "He's here, Patty."

For an instant she froze, unable to speak or breathe. A horrible, twisting pain stabbed at her chest. There was no need to ask whom he meant. Patty knew. With every tormented nerve end, she knew he meant Lije Masters.

"Where?" Her eyes fluttered closed to try to shut out the pain as she uttered the question in a choked voice.

"In the fourth row on your left." A touching sympathy laced his words. "His wife is with him."

A sob rose in her throat and Patty caught it back with a quick gulp. *Smile,* she commanded herself sternly, *smile and wave at him even if it kills you.* Some of her panic was communicated to the white horse and he shifted nervously beneath her.

Touching the silky neck with a soothing caress, Patty deliberately let her gaze stray to the fourth row of the stand. A smile of false surprise was forced onto her mouth as she met the pair of gray eyes looking at her from a lean, tanned face. The air of remoteness vanished as

14

he returned the smile, its effect still devastating to her heartbeat.

Her gaze flickered to the perfection of the blond woman beside him, envy squeezing nearly every ounce of breath from her lungs. That was Lije's wife, the perfect example of femininity. Not a tomboy turned into a cowgirl like Patty, she thought in self-deprecation. But she waved anyway.

"Magnificent performance as usual, Patty," Lije called to her.

"Thanks." The shrill edge of her voice was from pain.

There was a resounding slap on the rump of her horse as Everett King waved to the cowboys holding the front pair to take them to the stables. She and her grandfather were too close for Patty not to realize that his urgings were to end the conversation with the man she still loved and who had married another.

At the stables, **Patty** slipped from Loyalty's back and helped her grandfather, who had followed, to remove the leather trappings from the six white horses. Their travel trailer was parked a short distance away. A quick trip and Patty had changed out of her costume into faded blue Levi's and a knit top of olive green. She kept her movements swift and hurried, not allowing herself time to think in case she lost the grip on her shaky composure.

The horses were cooled off when she returned to the stable area. The shouts and applause from the rodeo crowd could be heard in the distance along with the rodeo announcer's voice. The sounds had all become familiar to her. Rodeo was her life, thanks to Lije Masters.

"I'll finish up the horses, grandpa," Patty said softly.

His alert brown gaze was turned on her thoughtfully, seeing beyond the composed facade to the pain beneath. "You want to be alone, don't you, honey?"

"Is it so obvious?" she smiled ruefully.

"Only to me," he responded as he walked away.

Patty watched his lean figure disappear and sighed. It was strange that he was the only member of her family who had seen the way she felt. Both her parents had assumed her interest in rodeo came from her grandfather, who had actively competed in his younger years. But her motivation had always been Lije Masters. Since the day she could remember, he had been the reason for her existence, all through her teenage years into adulthood.

When he had started following the rodeo circuit to save his father's ranch and keep it after his father's death, Patty had been determined to follow. She didn't have the patience to wait in New Mexico for the day he would return. It was her grandfather, Everett King, who had suggested trick riding, since her parents couldn't afford to support her as a barrel racer.

Fate, unfortunately, had taken a hand. Her bookings hadn't included the San Antonio rodeo. Liberty had been off-color and Patty had been at her parents' ranch in New Mexico before going to the Houston rodeo. She thought she would never lose the bitter taste that had coated her mouth the day she had walked into the restaurant in New Mexico and had seen Lije Masters with his new wife. To this day, she knew she had carried the scene off beautifully, never letting him see how crushing his news had been.

A tear slipped from her lashes as she needlessly pushed the straw around in Liberty's stall, using the pitchfork more for support. There was little comfort for her broken heart in reminding herself that Lije had never once given her any indication that he looked on her as anything more than a friend and neighbor. Still she had lived in hope. She had adored him, worshiped him, loved him, living on the smallest crumb of his attention for days.

Her hope had been nurtured by the knowledge that Lije didn't believe in riding the rodeo circuit and leaving his wife at home, nor in bringing her with him to go through the agonies of watching him compete, always knowing he was running the risk of being hurt or crippled. Yet she had lived with that fear for three years. Patty had known, too, that Lije had intended to quit after another two successful years of rodeo.

Never in her wildest imagination had she believed that he would fall in love and marry someone else in the space of three short days. But he had. It had been a year and a half ago since that fatal day, but the pain was as intense as if it had only happened this morning.

It was her grandfather's shoulder that had been drenched with her tears. He was the one who had convinced her to continue the circuit when she wanted to curl up and die. She enjoyed the circuit, the constant training that was necessary to keep the horses in top form. It kept her from dwelling too much on the impossibilities of her dream, but it was still work. And it was not the way she had envisaged spending the rest of her life.

Patty had wanted a home and children. Lije's children to be sure, and a ranch that she could help him run. She was as capable as any ranch hand around. That had always seemed a plus factor in her favor, a reason why Lije would choose her above anyone else. How wrong she had been! His wife was a fashion model who had never been on a horse in her life, city-born and city-bred. She, Patty, could have given him so much more.

The salty taste of tears covered her lips and she realized with a start that she was crying. That was something she hadn't done in over a year. Hiccuping back the sobs, Patty wiped her cheeks with the back of her hand. Liberty turned luminous brown eyes on her and nickered softly. It took all her willpower to resist the urge to fling her arms around the horse's neck and cry. Misery and self-pity dominated her senses and Patty didn't notice the darkening of the stall.

"There you are, Skinny." A low-pitched, faintly derogatory voice spoke from the doorway. "I thought I might find you in some dark hole, licking your wounds like a hurt animal."

After an initial start of surprise, cold anger held her motionless. Only one person called her Skinny.

"I don't know what you're talking about, Morgan Kincaid," Patty glared. "And I don't particularly care, so why don't you just get out of here?"

"I could have been mistaken," he drawled lazily. His tall, husky, broad-shouldered figure blocked out the light. "But it seemed to me that you turned white as your horses when you saw Lije in the stands."

Patty held his blue gaze for an instant, but its latent sharpness was too perceptive. "You were mistaken," she snapped, turning away to begin moving the pitchfork in the straw.

"I'm glad to hear that." The strong mouth moved into a smile. "Thinking the way I was that you were all tore up at seeing Lije again, I would have sworn that there were tears on your cheeks."

"That's absurd!" She kept her face averted. "It's only perspiration. I don't know where you got the idea that it would bother me to see Lije. He and I are good friends."

"Listen, Skinny." His voice was patiently indulgent. "Nearly everyone on the circuit knows that you thought you were in love with the guy."

"I can't control what people think." Any more than she could control the faint tremor in her statement.

"No, that's true," Morgan Kincaid agreed, a thumb hooked negligently in his belt as he watched her moving the straw around the horse's hooves.

20

Patty turned on him suddenly, unable to tolerate any more of his unsubtle cross-examination. "Shouldn't you be at the chutes making sure your precious rodeo stock is all right?"

"Sam is the chute boss. That's his job," he answered smoothly. "Aren't you curious why Lije came all this way to see a rodeo?"

"Why don't you tell me?" she responded in a tone seething with irritation.

"He wants to sell Blake Willians a young bull-dogging horse he trained. It seems he needs the money."

"What's so unusual about that?" Patty shrugged impatiently. "Name me a rancher who doesn't need cash money?"

"It isn't for the ranch that he wants the money." There was a watchful stillness in the blue eyes. "His wife is going to have a baby."

Patty had already accepted that it was more than a probability that some day Lije and his wife would have children. But for the announcement to come now — without any warning — and from Morgan Kincaid, a man she loathed and despised, was more than her poise could conceal. Her brown eyes widened in shock as she uttered a gasping cry of pain. Morgan Kincaid's gaze glittered sharply over her.

"Now why should that bother you? You and

Lije are only friends." His mocking statement held the fine edge of cutting steel. "You certainly don't look happy at the news. A stranger might think you were envious or jealous."

Her fingers tightened convulsively on the pitchfork handle. "You've said what you came here to tell me. Now get out!"

He didn't move as he stared at her thoughtfully through narrowed eyes. "The old wound opened up, did it? You still think you love the guy?"

"I never thought! I *knew* I loved Lije!" Unwillingly Patty raised her voice, no longer trying to pretend that she didn't care. She lifted the pitchfork to a threatening angle. "And if you don't get out of here, I'll run this through you!"

The sudden movement and the angry voices unsettled the white horse tied in the stall. There was a frantic whinnying as he pulled against the lead rope, twisting and turning his head, his hooves beating an in-place cadence on the stable floor.

"Easy, boy," Morgan Kincaid murmured soothingly, ignoring the pitchfork Patty had aimed at him to move to the horse's head. The animal continued bobbing nervously, eyes rolling, but Liberty responded to the reassuring voice and the gentle touch of the human hand.

"That isn't any way for a lady to talk, is it, feller?"

That instant of regret that Patty had felt at upsetting the sensitive and spirited horse was overtaken by a wave of self-pity.

"I'm not a lady," she asserted with false vigor and pride. "I never have been a lady."

Letting her statement slide by without comment, Morgan Kincaid ducked under the horse's neck and stood on the opposite side of the horse a few feet from Patty. The quiet tone of his incoherent murmurs eased her own raw nerve ends as well as Liberty's. At last the horse snorted and began nuzzling the hay in the manger. With a large, tanned hand trailing along the horse's withers and over his back, Morgan wandered slowly toward Patty.

His almost complete indifference to her put her instantly on guard, the slightly lowered pitchfork raising a fraction of an inch. Cautiously she watched him turn to face her, her gaze centering on the movement of his right hand.

"You remind me of a bantam hen my mother used to have." His eyes insolently inspected her slender form.

His right hand touched the brim of his sweat-stained hat, lifting it off to reveal the thick black hair. Distracted by the unhurried

23

movement of his right hand, Patty wasn't prepared for the lightning swiftness of his left as his fingers closed over the pitchfork handle and wrenched it easily from her grasp. She made one futile grab to recover it before she was intimidated by his height and breadth. The pitchfork was discarded with a lazy toss over the manger.

Her back was against the stall partitions. "What do you mean, a bantam hen?" she demanded, fighting the sudden leap of fear her heart made.

His fingers spread themselves against the wall near her head as he leaned slightly forward, mockery in the vivid blue color of his eyes.

"Puny and proud." Tilting his head to the side, he studied her wary and angry expression. "It fits, though. Puny, proud Patricia."

Staring at the massive chest and the strength etched in every rugged plane of his face, Patty felt puny and at a decided disadvantage. But the second part of his observation was just as accurate as her hand raised to slap that mocking expression from his mouth. Her wrist was halted by a steel vice midway to the target.

"I find you contemptible, do you know that?" When her hand failed, she lashed out with her tongue. "You are disgusting and loathsome!"

24

Long sooty lashes couldn't veil the sudden blazing look in his eyes. "You're too big to take over my knee," he declared grimly.

The forbidding line of his jaw moved closer. With a swiftness unexpected in a man of his size, Morgan Kincaid used his body weight to pin her against the stable wall. Seizing her chin between two fingers, he forced it up while his mouth closed hers in a hard, punishing kiss.

Patty struggled for as long as she could, fighting for the air he seemed determined to crush from her lungs. All her senses were drugged by his overpowering masculinity. In surrender, she lay passive in his arms, letting him do with her as he willed.

The lack of resistance eased the bruising pressure of his mouth as it became mobile and warmly persuasive against hers. There was a vague stirring deep inside Patty to respond with instinctive reaction of a female to a male. She had no need to fight back the traitorous weakness of her flesh as Morgan raised his mouth from hers.

"I can better understand a couple of things now," he drawled lazily, his face not more than an inch from hers, the warm moistness of his breath fanning her lashes. "I know why Jack thought you needed more practice and why Lije sought his satisfaction elsewhere rather

25

than take what you blatantly used to offer him. If I'd been in Lije's place, I would have taught you how to make love and taken your gift."

There was an underlying hint of portent that sent a shudder of inescapability tingling down Patty's spine. "If you had been in Lije's place, I never would have offered anything," she taunted huskily.

The cruel line of his mouth curved into a smile. "What are you going to do now that you've saved all your kisses for a man who belongs to someone else? Give them out as good-luck kisses?"

"Lije belongs to no one but himself." She deliberately ignored the last jeering question.

"Does that mean you're considering trying to break up his happy home?"

Lije didn't love her. He never had. To try to come between him and his beautiful wife would only succeed in making her look like an even bigger fool.

"I meant nothing of the kind," Patty denied in bitter defeat. She hunched her shoulders together, trying to twist free of his firm hold. "Will you let me go?"

"If I do, will you hit me or run into a corner to hide and try to remember Lije's kisses?"

"He was infinitely better at kissing than you!" She trembled violently with her dislike as

26

he laughed at her statement. The throaty sound was more infuriating than any mocking words. "What's the matter? Don't you think I know?" she demanded angrily. "He kissed me lots of times. They were always warm, gentle kisses, not coarse and animalistic like yours!" Her fingers touched her sore and tender mouth, still throbbing from his rough kiss while the skin around it was red and scraped by his shaven beard. "Your kisses hurt!"

"Love hurts." His narrowed blue gaze glittered down at her. "Or haven't you learned that?"

"I can't imagine you knowing anything about love," Patty retorted with contemptuous sarcasm.

"Hell!" Morgan chuckled in amusement, releasing her arms and stepping away. "I'm only thirty-five. I couldn't possibly know as much as you do! Why, you must be all of — what, twenty-two?"

If looks could kill, they would have been carving the date of his death on the gravestone as Patty glared her hatred of him.

"Yes, I am twenty-two," she asserted vigorously, "which hardly makes me an immature teenager, ignorant of the facts of life!"

"You may know about them, but you aren't on speaking terms." The grooves near his mouth deepened with mockery.

"I don't doubt that your bestial existence has given you intimate knowledge," Patty lashed back.

"Don't knock it if you haven't tried it, Skinny," Morgan winked.

In that fleeting second, she realized that he was deliberately provoking her temper for his own amusement, laughing at how quickly she rose to the bait.

"I have work to do, and I'm wasting my breath arguing with you." She spun away and stalked through the stall door toward the tack room.

"Need any help?" Morgan asked from the tack doorway.

Patty shook out Liberty's blanket, black with a white rose on the hip. "Never from you," she answered sarcastically.

"Suit yourself." There was an indifferent shrug of his broad shoulders as he turned away, then paused. "Are you going to Kelly's tonight?" he asked, referring to a local bar.

"No, I am not."

"Good. I've just won a hundred dollars."

"What are you talking about?" Patty frowned, giving Morgan her undivided attention.

"I bet gramps a hundred dollars that you wouldn't show up tonight because Lije and his

28

wife were going to be there," he responded in a complacent drawl.

"Gramps? You mean — my grandpa?"

"Who else? I tried to tell him you'd be too grief-stricken over meeting Lije again to go, but he kept insisting you were made of sterner stuff — smiling on the outside and crying on the inside type of thing. I don't believe he understands women as well as he thinks he does," Morgan concluded wryly. "Females enjoy being miserable."

Patty's mouth opened and closed. No words came to mind that were sufficiently sarcastic to give vent to her wrath. She was still searching for them as he walked away, heading toward the pens where the rodeo stock was held.

CHAPTER TWO

Everett King was seated at the small table in the travel trailer, studying a road map when Patty entered. The jacket of his light blue suit was lying on the back of a chair. His string tie was hanging loose and the top buttons of his white shirt opened. Running his gnarled fingers through his pepper gray hair, he glanced up and smiled.

"Do you have the horses all settled for the night?" he inquired.

"Grandpa, did you make a bet with Morgan Kincaid tonight?" She stopped beside the table, her hands on her hips, her head tilted to the side.

"Whatever gave you that idea?" There was a disbelieving look from his brown eyes before they returned to the study of the road map.

"Morgan Kincaid was the 'whatever' that gave me the idea," Patty answered grimly.

"You talked to him, did you?" Her grandfather breathed in deeply at her answering nod and folded up the map. "Are you going to Kelly's?" He didn't glance up as he asked the question.

"I shouldn't go, just to teach you a lesson," she sighed.

"But you are going," he stated positively, a decided twinkle in the brown eyes that met her pair of equally dark ones.

"You did it deliberately, didn't you, grandpa?" Her mouth curved into a smile of affectionate exasperation. "I'll bet you even told Morgan where I was just to make sure that I found out about it. You knew he wouldn't be able to resist the temptation of telling me."

"That sounds as if I tricked you into going," he said with mock reproval.

"You did and you know it!" Patty shook her head and stepped into the small kitchen area. "We can't afford to lose a hundred dollars on a silly bet like that and I couldn't stand a week of Morgan's gloating. I suppose he is the stock contractor at our next rodeo?"

"Well, yes, actually he is," her grandfather admitted reluctantly.

"Your little maneuver was successful," she sighed. "I am going to Kelly's, but you're going with me. I'll need some moral support — so don't you go off in some corner with Lefty."

"There's a towel and washcloth in the

31

shower," he told her. There was a pause as he darted her a twinkling glance and added, "And I laid your yellow outfit on the bed just in case you decided to go."

"Just in case, huh? Sometimes, gramps, you're positively exasperating!" Patty declared as she walked into the miniature bath area on the side of the trailer.

"I take after my granddaughter," he called after her.

Twenty minutes later she was tucking the opaque flowered blouse into the waistband of the matching lemon yellow slacks. Her dark brown hair was brushed free of its braid to hang loose and tickle her shoulder blades. The casual style alleviated the tomboy image, but the lightly applied lipstick, mascara and eyeshadow couldn't dim the youthfully open look to her features.

With a resigned shrug, Patty turned away from the mirror. She couldn't compete with the sophisticated perfection of the blond model who was Lije's wife. Althought she did have a grandfather who maneuvered her into impossible situations, she didn't have a fairy godmother who could suddenly transform her into a raving beauty with a wave of a wand.

Besides, hadn't she learned already that Lije didn't see her as anything more than the little girl next door? She wished she could despise him for the way she had wasted all those years waiting for him. It might make it easier to get over him. But she couldn't and didn't. She just kept right on loving him as thought nothing had changed.

"All right, grandpa," she said, as she walked through the tiny kitchen to the equally tiny living room of the trailer. "I'm ready. We'd better go before I change my mind."

His shirt was buttoned and his jacket back on. The Western string tie was secured in its longhorn clasp. He set his ivory tan stetson at a jaunty angle on his peppery dark hair.

"There aren't any quitters in the King family," he smiled, and opened the trailer door.

"I wish I were as sure about that as you are," Patty murmured as she followed him into the starlit night.

The churning of her stomach was worse than anything she had experienced prior to a performance as they approached the entrance of the small tavern a few blocks from the arena grounds. Because of its closeness, it was frequented by a majority of the rodeo cowboys, those who weren't flying elsewhere to compete in another rodeo. That majority seemed to be there in force tonight, Patty decided when she and her grandfather stepped through the doors.

The room was hazy with smoke, a gauze cloud that hung near the ceiling. The billiard tables in one corner were the scene of some good-natured baiting, the loud voices mixing with the laughter and chatter coming from the tables in the rest of the tavern. Overriding all of the din was a country dance band playing a popular song.

"Do you see him here?" Patty whispered nervously.

"He's sitting over by the dance floor. There's an empty table beside him. Come on," Everett King ordered.

Her searching eyes found Lije easily. He was facing the door with his arm resting on the back of his wife's chair. Blake Williams, one of the leading professional steer wrestlers, was seated at the table with him, for the present commanding Lije's attention.

But Patty wasn't interested in Blake Williams. All of her attention was centered on Lije, catching the loving glance he gave his wife. The look brought a stab of jealousy that cruelly twisted its blade in her heart. *What a striking couple they make,* she thought dejectedly. The thought didn't stop her from wishing that she had been the recipient of that glance.

Her grandfather's hand guided her along the edge of the dance floor. The chin that had begun drooping was jerked up as Patty looked into a pair of thoughtfully mocking blue eyes. She had been so intent on Lije that she hadn't noticed Morgan Kincaid among the dancers on the floor. But he was there, partnering Jill Van Wert, a tawny-haired barrel racer who followed the rodeo circuit just as the professional cowboys did. The pair had paused directly in their path.

"I see you've changed your mind," Morgan observed dryly.

"Yes, I did," Patty agreed with cold arrogance. "It looks as if you lose."

His metallic gaze flickered to her grandfather. "I guess so."

"Lije has just come in, Patty," Jill Van Wert inserted with a faintly catty edge to her tongue. "He's seated right over there − with his wife. Have you seen him yet?"

Patty's mouth tightened. She had never liked Jill very much. The girl was an excellent barrel racer, but Patty had always had the impression that it wasn't the competition that had prompted Jill to follow the rodeo, but the cowboys − in the plural sense.

"Yes, I did notice him," she answered stiffly. "Gramps and I were just on our way over to say hello."

"We mustn't keep you, then." Morgan smiled

35

crookedly, his eyes openly laughing at the stiff, defensive expression on her face. "See you later."

"What I wouldn't give to dance on that man's grave!" Patty muttered in a savage underbreath as Morgan Kincaid guided his attractive partner onto the dance floor again.

Everett King clicked his tongue at her in a reproving manner and started moving her toward Lije's table.

That spurt of anger at Morgan seemed to have eased some of her tension and brought the color into her cheeks. Gathering her courage, she commanded a bright expression to appear on her face as they neared the table.

"I'm still kicking myself for not buying that red horse of yours two years ago, Lije, when you sold him to Tod," Blake Williams was grumbling. "If I had, I'd be the one raking in the dough off him instead of Tod."

"Horses, horses, horses!" Patty forced herself to laugh. "It seems as if that's what you were talking about the last time I saw you, Lije."

"Hello, Patty, Everett." Lije rose to his feet to welcome them to the table. "It's good to see you again."

With a sinking heart, Patty noticed the easy warmth with which he greeted them. The cool aloofness was gone, no doubt melted by the ardent glow that was in his wife's eyes whenever she looked at him.

"Are you going to introduce me to this lovely lady, Lije?" her grandfather asked after shaking hands.

"Of course," Lije smiled. "This is my wife Diana." Patty wanted to cry at the caressing way he spoke her name. "Diana, I know you've met Patty King. This is her grandfather, Everett King."

The vacant table and chairs were pulled closer to include Patty and her grandfather in their small group. Patty found herself sitting next to the silvery blonde, who seemed more beautiful than Patty remembered. She felt like the ugly duckling next to the swan.

"That was a stunning performance you gave tonight," complimented Diana Masters with obvious sincerity. "I really envy your horsemanship, Patty."

Patty wondered what Diana's reply would be if she said that she envied Diana her husband. The fleeting glimpse of compassion that flickered through the blonde's luminous blue eyes gave Patty the impression that such a statement would not surprise Lije Master's wife. The last thing she wanted was Diana's pity.

"Thank you." Her mouth moved stiffly into a smile, so Patty turned her face away from the woman. "Actually my grandfather deserves much of the credit since he helps me with the training and perfecting the stunts."

"She's just as modest as she always was, Lije," Everett King grinned. "I may help, but you couldn't get me to stand on the backs of those two horses while I was trying to control the four ahead of them."

"And I'll bet Patty feels the same about those bulls you used to ride," Lije laughed.

"Either way, we're a team now," Patty inserted.

"Talking about a pair of Kings, I saw your family before Diana and I left. They told me to be sure to give both of you their love and to let you know all of them are fine. Your mother suggested that you could write more often, Patty," Lije smiled.

"She's right, I could," she sighed. "But I doubt if I will. You'd probably better carry the same message back from gramps and me."

"Well, Blake," her grandfather turned to the third man at the table, "I never have heard you say what you think of that bay horse Lije is trying to sell you."

"He's good," the man answered, turning his head to the side and smiling. "But I don't want to say how good for fear Lije will raise the price. We haven't started dickering yet."

With the topic changed to rodeo and horses, Patty was able to sit back and pretend an interest in the conversation.

The longer she sat, the tighter her chest seemed to constrict with pain at the sight of Lije's hand touching his wife's shoulder in light possession. Patty wondered if the ache in her heart would ever go away.

"Is this a private party or can anyone join?" The low, drawling voice belonging to Morgan Kincaid brought an immediate tensing of Patty's muscles.

"Pull up a chair and sit down, Morgan," Lije insisted.

There was an answering scrape of a chair leg behind Patty. Than a hand on the back of her chair was moving her to the side.

"Move over, Skinny," Morgan ordered with mock gruffness.

Flashing him a fiery look of irritation, Patty slid her chair away from Diana's. Every time he tormented her with that wretched nickname that he alone used, it made her feel like a bag of bones covered with a sack. Heaven knew she wasn't voluptuous, but her slender form did possess the necessary feminine curves.

His muscular shoulders and upper arms rubbed against her as he settled into the chair he had placed between the two women. Unconsciously Patty flinched from the contact and was punished for the withdrawal by the arm Morgan laid along the back of her chair. The mocking glitter in his gaze derided the resentment that darkened her eyes.

"This is quite a contrast," mused Morgan, glancing from Patty to the silvery blonde. "On one side I have the goddess Diana and on the other is a reincarnation of Annie Oakley."

A slow anger began to seethe to the surface. "And I thought you were going to make some remark about Beauty and the Beast, with you naturally being the Beast, Morgan," Patty smiled with poisonous sweetness.

"Careful, Skinny," he winked. "Your sarcasm is showing."

Lije leaned back in his chair, surveying the two of them with that indulgent look that had always filled Patty's heart with overwhelming admiration.

"Nothing has changed very much, has it?" Lije commented. "You two are still trading insults."

"I guess it's just a case of New Mexico water not being able to mix with Oklahoma oil," Morgan suggested lazily, sliding Patty a mocking look.

"I don't think I would have compared Patty with water," Diana spoke hesitantly. "Maybe

40

air — like a warm, summer day."

"No, it's water," Morgan assured her. "Placid and serene on the surface with treacherous undercurrents below. Besides, she's still wet behind the ears."

"Well, you're just like oil — slimy!" Patty retorted.

"Which makes me hard to catch. That's how I've managed to stay a bachelor." Her gibe slid away without causing any ripple of reaction on his smooth exterior.

"I thought two years ago you said it was going to be your last season on the rodeo circuit, Morgan," Lije commented. "Your brother Alex was going to take over the stock contracting part of your operations, wasn't he?"

"I considered quitting seriously for a while," Morgan shrugged indifferently, "but as you can see, I changed my mind."

What a pity, Patty thought silently.

As if reading her thoughts, Morgan darted her a knowing glance, showing his amusement at her dislike of him.

A calloused brown hand clamped itself on Lije's shoulder. "Ya sold Blake that hoss yet?" Lefty Robbins asked gruffly.

"I'm trying," replied Lije.

"Hello, Lefty," Diana smiled, tilting her head to look up to the short, wiry cowboy standing

41

behind her husband. Her blue gaze danced to the white cast on his left arm. "How did you break your arm this time?"

"Ah, one of Morgan's buckin' horses squeezed my arm in the chute. My bones are gettin' so brittle, they break if ya look at 'em cross-eyed." His leathery face was cracked by a smile. "Hey, congratulations! I heard you're gonna have an addition to yore family, Lije!"

An incredible proud light gleamed in the gray eyes that exchanged an intimate look with his wife. "That's right," Lije admitted.

"Congratulations," Patty forced the acknowledgment through the tight lump in her throat. "I – I hope you have a healthy and happy baby."

"Thank you," Diana returned sincerely, taking Lije's hand and holding it. "That's all either one of us is asking."

"Instead of congratulatin' someone else," Lefty spoke up, "you should be getting married and havin' one of your own, Patty. Don't you think so?"

The corners of her mouth trembled as she tried to make them curve into a smile. "I'm afraid I'm not the marrying kind, Lefty." With Patty, it was all or nothing, and if she couldn't have Lije, nothing was what she wanted.

"Well, Skinny, if you're not the marrying

42

kind, are you the dancing kind?"

Morgan Kincaid didn't give her a chance to reply as he pried her fingers free of the knots she had twisted them into and spun her out of the chair. Before she could plant her feet, he was pushing her onto the dance floor.

"If you call me Skinny one more time, I'll break a beer bottle over your head!" she threatened in a hissing undertone, and tried to pull her arm free of his iron grip. "And I don't want to dance with you!"

"I never asked whether you wanted to or not," he replied calmly, winding an arm around her slim waist. "You should be thanking me for saving you from some considerable embarrassment."

"What are you talking about?" Patty demanded.

Still holding her hand, he raised it with his to flick a finger on the end of her lower lash, touching the tear that trembled on the edge.

"Right now you're so busy hating me that you've forgotten you were about to cry." His mouth moved into a complacent smile.

"I was not," Patty denied. "And I should think you would have laughed if I had."

"You can't see me as the knight in shining armor, is that it?" he mocked. The hand on her back forced her to follow his steps.

43

"No I can't," she answered with obvious challenge as she kept her palm spread against his chest, trying to keep as much distance between them as possible.

"The truth is I wouldn't have cared if you'd embarrassed yourself or not." The ebony dark head was tilted to the side, a faint arch to one brow while the cold steel of his eyes contradicted the crooked smile on his mouth. "I am fond of your granddad, though. Since I'd already lost my bet, I was more concerned that your quivering 'stiff upper lip' would collapse and he would be left with the red face. Are you satisfied, Skinny? You were partially right."

She believed what he said was true, but the last gibe jarred the boiling cup of her anger. Snapping brown eyes burned a hole in the collar of his shirt, which was opened to reveal the muscular column of his throat.

Gritting her teeth, she retorted caustically, "Don't call me Skinny! I've outgrown my training bra."

"Have you?"

the taunting edge of laughter was in his voice. He moved her slightly away from him, his mocking gaze insolently inspecting her torso with embarrassing thoroughness before it returned to the flaming heat in her face. "And stop looking at me like that. It's insulting!" Patty hissed.

"You're a prude, Patty King," Morgan chided.

"Why?" she challenged angrily. "Because I don't like men disrobing me with their eyes?"

The grooves around his mouth deepened. "You'd better keep your voice down."

Self-consciously Patty glanced around the small dance floor, her eyes seeing the amused looks that were being directed at them. She wanted to squirm like a butterfly on a pin, but she wouldn't give Morgan that satisfaction.

"You're insufferable," she murmured quietly. "You enjoy making me look a fool."

"You dig your own hole," Morgan responded dryly. "I just watch."

Long ago she had stopped hearing the music, letting her feet automatically follow his lead. So when the song ended, her feet kept moving until she bumped into the broad wall of his chest. Before Patty could regain her balance and step back, his arm had tightened around her waist.

"The song is over. Will you please let me go?" Patty demanded coldly.

"Where will you go? The party has disbanded, so you won't want to go back to the table."

The band began playing another slow tune.

45

The hand on her back firmly guided her to follow his steps, turning her at a slight angle so she could see the table where Lije was seated. Only he, Diana and Blake Wiliams were there.

"Where's grandpa?" she asked, tearing her gaze from the fingers Lije had laced through his wife's as the two hands rested on the tabletop, the tenderly intimate contact there for all to view.

"He's playing a game of checkers with Lefty," Morgan informed her. "I suppose you could go back to the table. While Lije and Blake discuss his horse, you could help Diana pick out some names for the baby."

"Stop it!" The desperate command was issued in an underbreath taut with pain.

The natural direction of their steps turned her away from the table. With a start, Patty discovered that her fingers had been digging into the solid muscle of Morgan's shoulder. Instantly she relaxed the grip. As she did so, some of the fight drained out of her.

"So you've condemned yourself to following the rodeo circuit the rest of your life, have you?" Morgan commented.

"What?" Patty asked faintly, not really following his statement.

"At the table, you said you weren't the marrying kind," he reminded her. "We both know it's

46

really a case of 'if you can't be Mrs. Masters, you don't want to marry anyone.' Since you don't intent to marry and settle down, that only leaves you the circuit."

"I was thinking about opening a Roman riding school in a few years," Patty shrugged, for some reason unable to take offense at his gibes.

"And where have you planned to locate it? In New Mexico? On your parents' ranch? Next door, so to speak, to Lije?" Morgan jeered softly. "Are you hoping that after a few years the luster will wear off his wedding band?"

A weary frown creased her forehead. "I'm tired, Morgan. Will you please leave me alone?"

His usually mocking features were drawn in serious, thoughtful lines. "I imagine you'd like to go home."

Patty didn't answer, but her gaze swung to the side table where her grandfather and Lefty Robbins were bent over the checkerboard. Their games were inevitably grudge matches that could go on for hours. Morgan had followed her gaze.

"I'll take you back."

Immediately she stiffened. "No, thank you. I'll take the truck and grandpa can find his own way to the trailer."

"It will be the wee hours of the morning before they break up," Morgan stated firmly. "They'll either have to walk or take a taxi back to the grounds."

"I don't want *you* to take me," Patty declared, pushing her weight against the iron hand on her back. "Besides, Jill will be furious if you leave with me."

"I can't imagine Jill being jealous of you."

"Thanks a lot!" she hurled sarcastically. "You're really great for a person's ego!"

The song ended and he laughed down at her. "I only meant that she knows how much you despise me. She'll hardly think that you and I will be sneaking off to indulge in some passionate rendezvous. Chances are I'll be back before she realizes I had left, unless you were considering a few consoling kisses?"

"Don't be disgusting!"

Spinning away from the loosened hold on her waist, Patty weaved through the tables to the exit, only to have Morgan's hand reach around her to open the door.

Her mouth tightened as she walked out of the door, his long, broad shadow falling over her, blocking out the light from the bar. She took one step in the direction of her own pickup and his hand curved around the back of her neck, his fingers enmeshed in her long hair.

"You're riding with me, Skinny," Morgan announced.

Turning as much as the punishing hand on her neck would allow, Patty glared into the roughly masculine face, midnight black hair curling down toward thick black brows. The blue of his eyes was lost in the dark of the night and the lazily narrowed sooty lashes. The calmly determined set of his jaw irritated her.

"I have no wish to ride with you," she declared frostily.

"We aren't talking about wishes. You have three choices. We can stand out here and argue. You can go with me peaceably or I can carry you. Now, which is it going to be?"

Their eyes locked in silent challenge. "I wish I were a man," Patty sighed bitterly, breaking away from his gaze as tears of angry frustration filled her eyes.

"There you go, talking about wishes again," he mocked.

His fingers released her neck and twined themselves deeper in her hair, tugging it sharply to send shooting fires of pain through her scalp. Uselessly she grabbed for his arm in self-protection.

"You're a brute! Do you know that?" she accused.

His expression was calm and unruffled. "I know you think so. What's it going to be — do I carry you or are you walking?"

The thought of being crushed unwillingly against that massive chest the second time in one day sent waves of heat flowing through her blood. The last time was much too vivid in her mind for Patty to want a repeat performance. That was an experience she wanted to forget.

"If you would quit pulling my hair, I'll walk to your stupid truck!" Patty muttered.

"Was I pulling it?" Morgan asked with false innocence. Untangling his fingers, he smoothed the hair from the back of her neck to her shoulders. "I'm so used to seeing you in your Annie Oakley pigtails that I was probably subconsciously making certain these silky locks were yours and not a wig."

"You wanted me to cry uncle and you know it!" she bit savagely, twisting away from his hand and stalking toward his blue truck.

"I was paying you a compliment." Again a door was opened before Patty could reach it, this time the door of the truck.

"Save them for the other girls who are bowled over by your potent male virility," she retorted. "Personally, I find it revolting!"

Morgan walked around the truck, slamming the door as he slid behind the wheel. "Don't worry, Skinny." He turned the key in the ignition and the motor growled to life. "I'm not trying to compete with Lije or his memory for your favors."

"His memory?" Involuntarily, Patty shuddered. "You make it sound as if he's dead."

"For you, he is."

Patty stared at the profile etched against the side window of the truck, the slanting forehead, the strong straight nose, the firm mouth and jutting chin. There was a sinking sensation in the pit of her stomach. As much as she hated to admit it, Morgan Kincaid was right.

If she truly wanted to get over Lije, she had to bury the past, all her love, memories and dreams. They had been a part of her for so long, it would be like cutting off an arm or a leg. The question was did she want to let go of them and let Lije become only a long-time friend and neighbor?

Sobered and frightened by the decision she discovered she had to make for her future, a troubled light entered her chocolate brown eyes. She had been living one day at a time. Now, thanks to Morgan, she was forced to look farther ahead.

"Has the cat got your tongue?" Amusement teased the corners of the firm mouth.

Blinking into the pair of eyes that didn't

appear nearly as blue in the shadows, Patty realized the truck was stopped and the motor switched off. She glanced around in confused surprise, recognizing the rodeo grounds and the trailer they were parked beside. It seemed only just an instant ago that Morgan had turned the truck into the street outside the bar.

The hint of a smile was gone from Morgan's face. "What's the matter, Pat?"

"Nothing's the matter," she answered in a taut voice. "I was daydreaming, that's all."

Frantically her hand searched for the door handle, needing to escape. The latch clicked and Patty started to push the door open. Morgan's arm reached around her. His hand found the armrest and pulled it shut. Her senses that had been deadened by the misery induced by her thoughts flamed to awareness.

His fingers maintained their grip on the armrest while the hard muscles of his arm acted like an iron band across her breasts to keep her in her seat. The thin, synthetic material of her blouse transmitted his searing body heat to her soft flesh.

"I accepted your ride home. Now will you please let me get out?"

Tongues of charged lightning licked along her spine as she made her haughty demand.

His rough, masculine face was close, narrowed blue eyes studying her features, focusing at last on the mutinous set of her lips. One side of his mouth quirked upward at the corner.

"You aren't as skinny as I thought," Morgan commented blandly.

Patty had tolerated the arm across her breasts because she hadn't wanted to draw attention to the uncomfortable intimacy of his touch. Foolishly, she thought he hadn't noticed. A bright glitter sparkled in his eyes as she tried to push him away.

"I was only going to take a kiss for luck," he chuckled.

"Take it," she challenged with cold defiance. "It will only bring you bad luck."

His thumb forced her chin up as Morgan accepted her challenge. Warm breath touched her lips an instant before his mouth claimed hers. Flash fire raced through her veins, quickly burning itself out when the firm pressure was lifted from her lips. Resentment smoldered in the look she gave him.

"Happy nightmares." Morgan winked good-humoredly, and without another word clicked open the door and slid back behind the wheel.

CHAPTER THREE

Unwrapping the last of the protective leg cottons from the white horse's leg, Patty straightened, arching her back to relieve the fatigue of the long drive. The travel days in between rodeos always seemed much longer than other days with so much preparation to be done before leaving and upon arrival at their destination.

After affectionately stroking Legend's silken neck, Patty gathered the cotton and bandages and walked to the tack compartment of the goose-necked horse trailer. The crunch of footsteps on the gravelly sand sounded behind her and she glanced over her shoulder.

"Hi, grandpa. Are you all done or do you need some help?" she asked.

"I'm all done except for Liberty," he answered, a look of tired concern on his tanned, ageless face. "I thought the roads were smooth enough that we didn't need to apply any cold water midway through the trip, but I guess the long haul was too long. There's a slight swelling in his legs."

"Thank heaven we don't have a performance tonight," Patty sighed. "Do you want me to help rub him down?"

"No." Everett King waved aside her offer. "Go put on a pot of coffee and get our trailer straightened around."

"That sounds like a grand idea," Patty agreed with weary enthusiasm, handing the leg wrappings to her grandfather to put away.

As Patty left the stabling area and headed toward their travel trailer, the blare of a semi-trailer horn tooted behind her. Her steps slowed to wait for the large truck to pass. The stock trailer behind the tractor was emblazoned with the words Kincaid Rodeo Company. There was a shifting of gears as the truck rolled alongside her.

"Hello, Princess. Where are you off to?" The truck slowed to a stop while the cowboy driver stuck his head out of the window, the wide-brimmed white hat tilted at a cocky angle to reveal waving light brown hair.

"Hi, Jack!" Patty returned gaily, her feet moving lightly over the ground as she moved toward the cab of the truck. "Just heading to the trailer to fix some coffee."

"You have your horses all settled in, huh?"

he asked rhetorically, and motioned toward the back end of the truck. "I'll be getting rid of my cargo of bulls pretty soon myself."

"When did you start driving for Morgan?" She stood on the running board to raise herself to his level.

"Since I finished out of the averages at the last four rodeos and discovered my pockets were empty," Jack Evans grinned.

"That's what you get for looking at the girls in the short skirts sitting in the box seats instead of paying attention to the bucking horse you're riding," Patty teased.

A boyish look filled with appealing charm stole across his face. "What I really need is a sweet, steady girl to keep me in line. Why don't you volunteer for the job, Princess? We'd make a great combination."

"If I ever took your flirting seriously, Jack Evans, you would fly out of here as fast as a horse that's just backed into an electric fence," Patty replied lightly.

"I wouldn't be too sure about that." He cocked his head to the side in denial as his gaze roamed over her face and the dimples in her cheeks. "The more I keep looking into your baby brown eyes and seeing that image of slippers and pipe, the more inviting it becomes."

A pair of large strong hands nearly circled Patty's waist from behind as she was lifted from the running board and set on the ground, despite her startled outcry of protest.

"Sorry to end your charming little scene, Skinny." Morgan Kincaid's voice carried no apologetic tone. "But I have to get those bulls unloaded and settled in."

"You could have said so!" Patty retorted, recovering with angry swiftness from her surprise. "You didn't have to manhandle me!"

The smile he gave her was cold. "You haven't been manhandled enough to know the meaning of the word."

Then the steel gaze was turned to the cowboy already shifting the truck back into gear. "Get that truck up to the pens, Jack."

"Right away, Morgan," Jack Evans agreed cheerfully, addressing a one-fingered salute to Patty. "See you later, Princess."

"What are you princess of?" There was a harsh, mocking look in the eyes Morgan turned to her. "Ice or snow?"

Since that night more than a week ago, Patty had deliberately ignored Morgan, responding with chilling civility only if he addressed her directly.

"You'll have to ask Jack," she answered sarcastically.

57

"I wondered how long it would take Jack to get around to giving you the rush," he mused thoughtfully. "He's made the rounds with nearly all the other girls on the circuit."

"Look who's talking!" There was a haughty arch to her finely drawn brow.

The action seemed to amuse him. "I'd love to stand here and argue with you, if only to keep in practice. Unfortunately I have other things to do." He took her by the shoulders and turned her around to face her trailer. With an insulting slap on her rump, he sent her on her way. "Get along home, Skinny. You'll have to sharpen your tongue on me another day."

There had been a sting to his slap and Patty had to resist the desire to rub the smarting area. She spun around to fling a last poisonous dart at him and discovered his long strides had already taken him several yards away in the direction of the semi-trailer truck.

With her target practically out of range, she pivoted sharply toward the trailer, her unvented temper adding haste to her footsteps. She cursed herself for letting Morgan get under her skin the way she did.

It was that all-knowing attitude of his that irritated her, that and the way he laughed at her. All she had to do was see him and the happiest song would hit a sour note.

After the coffeepot was filled with coffee and water, Patty set it on the gas burner of the small stove and began putting back the breakable items she had packed away before the morning's journey. She was in the bedroom setting the clock on the small shelf near the bed when her grandfather came in.

"The coffee isn't quite done yet," she called out to him. "Do you want to shower and change while you wait?"

"No, I don't think so," he answered.

"I think I will," speaking her thoughts aloud without actually addressing her comment to him. She ran a hand over her hair. "And wash my hair, too."

"You go ahead, girl," nodded her grandfather as she stepped from the bedroom into the narrow hallway and opened the door containing the bath towels. "I'll have to check on Libbie later on. After that I'll clean up."

Patty leaned against the closet, drawing her brows together in a serious expression. "Gramps, there's something I've been meaning to talk to you about."

"Do you want to save it for another time, honey?" he asked as he bent his lean frame to peer out of the window of the trailer. "Pete Barber just walked by and I wanted to talk to him about when we can use the arena tomorrow for practice. We'll discuss it later, okay?"

With a wave of his hand, he was walking out the door.

With a shrugging sigh, Patty hung the bath towels on the rack beside the shower stall, walked into the small kitchen to turn down the fire under the bubbling coffee pot and returned to adjust the water temperature for her shower. A few minutes later she was beneath the refreshing spray, the tingling jets of water massaging her tired muscles as it and the soap washed her clean.

She had just lathered her hair when she heard the trailer door open and her grandfather walk in again. "The coffee is done. You can pour yourself a cup now."

Ducking her head under the spray to rinse away the shampoo, Patty called out again. "The thing I wanted to talk to you about was next year's bookings. I'd like to change our tour to another circuit."

"Why?" was his answering question.

Her hair squeaked clean and she turned off the water, stepping from the shower to wrap her head in one towel as she dried herself with the other.

"I know all the arguments for staying here," she replied. "It's closer to home. The dates are all fairly close, so we don't have very many long trips to make from one rodeo to the other. And we've performed in all these places before so they know us and it's easier to book. But I think it's time we made a change, saw a different part of the country."

She paused, staring at the wall as if she could see through it to the kitchen on the other side. Her mouth twisted wryly.

"The truth is I want to get away from all these old faces, all the people that have known me since I started in the business. They all remember me as that pigtailed little kid that followed Lije around. And I'm tired of their amused sympathy."

An angry toss of the towel onto the rack followed the last clipped statement. "Especially Morgan Kincaid! I know you like him, but I really can't stand him!"

Reaching for the robe that she usually kept on the bathroom hook, Patty discovered it wasn't there. The clink of a cup against a saucer sounded from the kitchen as she reached for the damp towel on the rack and wrapped it sarong-wise around her body.

"Before you start telling me all the reasons why it's impossible to switch circuits, pour me a cup of coffee," she called out.

Her grandfather's muffled okay was followed by movements in the kitchen and another clink of a cup while Patty wiped up the scattered droplets of water that had escaped from the shower. She and her grandfather had discussed the possibility of changing their tour before, shortly after Lije was married. At the time she had been too miserable to argue and had been easily persuaded by his arguments to stay with the same circuit. Now she felt distinctly refreshed and ready to do battle. He would find that she wouldn't be so easily convinced this time!

As she stepped from the small bathroom into the equally small hallway, a cup of coffee was held out to her.

Patty froze at the sight of the large hand that held it, her gaze springing to its owner. The searing flames in her cheeks were not the result of the warm shower, but from the appraising look Morgan Kincaid was giving her as he inspected her from bare head to bare toe, taking his leisure to study all the bareness the towel exposed in between.

"What are you doing here? Where's grandpa?" Patty breathed, unable to meet the bright gleam in his eyes or see past the massive shoulders to the living area of the small trailer.

"Outside, talking to Pete." The hand holding the cup moved forward. "Don't you want your coffee now?"

With fumbling fingers, she took the cup from him, her knees quivering at the familiar and insulting way he kept looking at her. The warmth from the cup was comforting and she wrapped her fingers around it to draw strength.

"Was that you I heard come into the trailer? Grandpa didn't −" Her voice began to tremble, too.

"Gramps didn't hear a word you said. You'll have to repeat your carefully rehearsed speech again," Morgan smiled at her with infuriating complacency.

"You knew I thought it was grandpa out here. You could have let me know," she accused resentfully.

"I didn't find out anything that I didn't already know, so what's the harm?" One shoulder was lifted in a mocking shrug.

"There is no harm. I can't stand you, and I'll gladly say it to your face!" Patty retorted. "But it was supposed to be a private conversation. If you had any manners or sense of decency, you would have let me know you were here." She placed a hand on her hip in rigid challenge. "Exactly why are you here?"

"I wanted to talk to you and gramps together," Morgan replied easily, the glitter never leaving the sapphire depths of his eyes. "He was busy with Pete, so he suggested that I come in here and wait. The coffee was your idea. Incidentally, you make very good coffee."

"I wish you'd choke on it!" Patty hissed, spinning away to stalk to her bedroom in the rear of the trailer, the spurt of temper giving strength to her previously unsteady legs.

"So you've decided to run, have you?" Morgan drawled.

"It is not running!" she answered vehemently. "It's a new start." She stopped short beside her bed, stamping a bare foot in frustration. "I don't know why I'm explaining my reasons to you. It's none of your business!"

"I don't suppose so," he agreed lazily.

Whether it had been the furious pounding of blood in her ears or a subconscious belief that Morgan wouldn't follow her or a combination of both, Patty hadn't heard the footsteps following her to the bedroom. Not until his voice came from inside the doorway did she realize he was behind her.

"Get out of my bedroom!"

The towel almost slipped loose when she pivoted sharply around. The quick movement of her hand saved her from an embarrassing incident.

"Is this yours?" His gaze swung with casual interest around the small cubicle. "I didn't know if you or your grandfather slept here."

"Grandpa sleeps on the couch. I want to get dressed. Will you leave?"

Her teeth were grinding together as her nerves reacted to his dark form that nearly filled the room. The force of his masculinity was overpoweringly apparent.

"It's a shame that you wear jeans all the time," he commented, ignoring her biting order. "They cover up a very attractive pair of legs. They're very nicely shaped."

His lazy glance moved from the bareness of her thighs to the shadowy cleft between her breasts, partially visible above the towel wrapped around her body. "— Along with other things," Morgan added suggestively.

A crimson flush tinted her cheeks as she hitched the towel higher. The protective gesture drew a smile on the hard male mouth.

"I have to get dressed," Patty repeated, less vigorously than before as a nervous awareness took hold of her.

"Don't mind me." he shrugged.

The casual step he took farther into the room prompted Patty to take an immediate step backward. Her complete concentration on his presence blocked out the memory of how close she was to the bed. She backed into it, lost her balance, and started to fall onto its softness.

Morgan's reflexes were swifter. With lithe

coordination, a saving arm was circled around her waist while his other hand removed the spilling cup of hot coffee from hers.

The next breath she took, she found herself being held closely against his chest, the towel around her wet hair brushing his tanned cheek. The rough denim material of his Levi's was rubbing against her thighs while one of her hands clutched the cotton material of his shirt and the other had a death grip on the towel.

Drawing a shaky breath, Patty tilted her head back to meet the amused glitter shining through the smoky veil of his half-closed lashes. The pressure of the hand against the small of her back increased to arch her closer. Her coffee cup was now sitting on the shelf near her bed and his free hand moved slowly up her arm to caress a smooth white shoulder.

Her heart gave a frightened leap as she noticed the deliberately slow descent of his mouth. Twisting her head out of its path, she gasped at the provocative touch of his lips along her neck. Flames of sensuous delight licked her skin, emanating from the sensitive area he was exploring.

"Let me go," she breathed, erratically, afraid to struggle too vigorously and loosen the precarious hold on her bath towel.

"Kissing you seems to have become a habit

with me lately," he murmured against her neck.

"It's a bad habit," Patty answered in an angry whisper, fighting the involuntary shudders quaking to her toes.

Her head was twisted as far to the side as it could go, but his slowly searching mouth was making its way surely to hers. She tried to elude him by turning her face to the opposite side, an action Morgan had anticipated. His hand was there to halt her chin so the drugging warmness of his mouth could find hers.

The possessive firmness of his kiss acted like a hallucigen as a psychedelic display of rainbow colors exploded in her mind. Patty resisted the fascinating pull of the whirling display just as she resisted the pressure of his hands and the expert persuasion of his mouth.

The awkwardness of maintaining her scanty attire kept her attempts weak and unsuccessful. Only when Morgan chose to end the embrace was she allowed to pull free.

Wide, accusing eyes snapped their displeasure as she put a hasty step between them. The direction of the movement was toward the hallway door so she could escape should he try to approach her again. Her jerky, uncoordinated move had loosened the tuck she had made to keep the towel around her. When she tried to refasten it and watch Morgan at the same time, her fingers turned into thumbs of awkwardness.

"Here, kid, let me do that for you," Morgan said grinning.

"Don't you come near me!" she warned in a husky voice, clutching the loosened towel with both hands.

But he took a step toward her anyway, catching her by the waist with a second step when she turned to run down the hallway. She twisted and wiggled to be free, kicking at him with her bare feet and encountering only the hard leather of his cowboy boots.

"If you don't stop it," a gleam of amused indulgence glittered in his face despite the firmness in his voice, "I'm going to throw you on that bed. Now, stand still."

Patty started to ignore his command and continue her struggles, until she felt his hands on her waist and her feet being lifted from the floor.

"All right!" she said, gasping out her agreement in a panicked voice.

Morgan set her on the floor. "You're the hardest person in the world to help." His large hands retained their grip on her waist as he expected her to start fighting him again.

"Nobody likes to accept help from people they don't like," Patty jeered. "And if you were truly interested in helping me and not embarrassing me, you would leave this room and give me privacy to get dressed."

An uncaring shrug moved the shoulders in front of her. "You may be right. I'll try to remember that the next time something like this occurs."

Patty breathed in sharply in anger, ready to issue a cutting retort, only to have her breath stolen as he pulled the edges of the towel from her fingers. His movements were swift and sure. Before she could recover from her surprise, the towel was firmly in place. The tingling warmth in the breast he had accidentally touched sent hot flames of embarrassment up her neck.

"You're all cinched up again," Morgan laughed sensuously. "Do you feel better?"

"I won't feel better or safe until you're out of my sight!" she retorted.

The grooves remained around his mouth as his gaze narrowed on her face. The hand that had been negligently hooked in his waistband moved to capture her chin.

"I'd hate to have you find out you're wrong about thinking that way," he murmured.

Her fingers closed over the steel sinews in his wrist, trying to push his hand away from her chin. Then the firm pressure of his mouth was against hers, lingering and warm. Patty halted her useless efforts to push his hand away and worked on the strong chin and powerful jaw.

"Well, well, well, what's going on here?" The curious, laughing question of her grandfather relaxed Morgan's hold and Patty wrenched her face away.

There was nothing hurried or guilty in Morgan's actions as he turned toward her grandfather. "You should have come in sooner. A minute ago, Patty was in danger of losing her towel!"

"Will you tell him to get out of my bedroom?" Her voice shook with frustration, anger and humiliation.

"That sounds like her grandmother's rolling-pin voice," Everett King chuckled. "You'd better retreat while you're still in one piece, Morgan."

Before leaving, Morgan ran a finger across a crimson cheek, pushing the tip of her slightly tilted nose, then pulling it quickly away so her hand slashed impotently through thin air.

"Get some clothes on," he said, issuing a mock order. "Girls shouldn't run around like that in front of men. It can give them ideas."

"Get out of here, Morgan Kincaid!" Patty threatened, her powerless temper bringing her close to tears. "Get out of here before

I scream the walls down!"

He met her glaring gaze and winked. "It's all right, Skinny. I'm going right now, but you really don't have to put on an act for your grandfather's benefit."

She stared at his retreating broad back in speechless fury. How dared he insinuate to her grandfather's listening ears that she had enjoyed his kisses? Nothing could have been further from the truth and he knew it! With an angry exhalation of breath, Patty slammed the door, stomping to the small closet to yank out some clothes to wear.

As she dressed, she heard their quiet voices filtering into her room from the opposite end of the trailer. With her clothes on and the towel removed from her wet hair, the voices faded, the outside door opened and closed three times. Once the snarls were combed out of her hair, Patty walked to the door, listened silently and heard nothing. Morgan was gone.

Or so she thought until she walked into the hallway and saw the ebony blackness of his hair against the ivory curtains at the window behind the couch. The roughly carved face was turned toward her, knowing blue eyes holding her frozen look. When his gaze released her to lazily sweep over her denim jeans and checked blouse, Patty pivoted back toward her bedroom, determined not to endure his insufferable presence another second.

"Patty, come in here." her grandfather called out loudly.

"What for?" Her hand remained poised on the doorknob to her room, and she did not turn around to meet the laughing glitter that she knew would be in Morgan's eyes.

"Do you remember where I put your résumé? I've looked everywhere and can't find it." The shifting of papers muffled his reply.

"It's in the folder with those publicity photographs," she answered tautly.

"I can't find that either," sighed Everett King. "I don't know where you hide things in this darn trailer!"

"Can't I look for it later?"

The faintly desperate ring to her voice prompted a throaty chuckle from Morgan. "What she means, gramps, is after I leave."

Patty whirled around, dislike flashing in her eyes. "Yes, that is exactly what I mean!"

"This is business, Patty," her grandfather inserted with calm firmness. "There's no room for childish tantrums in business. Morgan wants to take the résumé with him when he leaves."

The quiet reprimand unwillingly moved her feet toward the tiny living room. "Why does he need it?" she challenged defiantly.

It was Morgan who replied instead of her grandfather. "A feature writer for the local newspaper wants to do an in-depth article on rodeo life and the people and animals who take part. Since your speciality act follows the circuit, I thought I'd get some background material on you."

"Morgan plans to meet the reporter tonight," her grandfather added, "and I've arranged it so he can interview you tomorrow after you've practised."

"By supplying the background material about your age and experience beforehand, it should save a lot of needless questions at the interview," Morgan explained.

It was difficult to dispute the logic of their arguments, as much as Patty wanted to, if only to thwart Morgan. The corners of her mouth were pulled grimly downward in resignation as she walked to the small bureau against the wall near her grandfather. Flipping through papers stacked on the shelf, she quickly found the folder containing the information Morgan wanted. Without a word, she handed it to her grandfather and retreated to the kitchen.

"That should do it," Morgan said crisply, and Patty knew her grandfather had given him the résumé.

She kept her back to the two men as she heard Morgan get to his feet and walk to the outside door. The tingling along the back of her neck said that he was looking at her.

"I'll be going now," he said in a mocking undertone. "I know how anxious Patty is to talk to you about her decision, Everett."

Stiffening angrily, she heard her grandfather's curious voice ask, "Her decision?"

"She's decided that this circuit isn't big enough for the two of us. Next year she wants you to book her on a different one." Morgan explained with open amusement.

Gritting her teeth, Patty glared over her shoulder at his masculine countenance. "I have a half notion to stay just to make your life as miserable as you make mine, except that I'm tired of getting sick to my stomach every time I look at you!"

His gaze narrowed even as his mouth curved into a mirthless smile. "It's been hell knowing you, too, Skinny."

He then flicked a look at her grandfather. "I'll see you later, Everett."

Her fingers dug into the edge of the kitchen counter, an unaccountable tightness in her throat at the sound of the door closing behind Morgan. Patty liked to be liked by others. Although she despised Morgan Kincaid, there was an odd little hurt that he should dislike her with equal fervor.

"What's all this about, Patty?" her grandfather asked gently.

"I simply can't stand it anymore!" She shook her head vigorously. "Everywhere we go, *he's* there! Tormenting me, making fun of me, ordering me around."

"You don't exactly turn the other cheek." There was a brief lifting of his brow in affectionate reproval.

"No, I don't," Patty sighed. "I don't mind so much being called Skinny and Annie Oakley and kid. I know I'm not a raving beauty even if I am fairly attractive. But I can't stand it when he starts tormenting me about Lije. The wounds never get a chance to heal."

"Maybe he's just trying to make sure all the poison is out so they'll heal without leaving a scar," her grandfather suggested.

"Morgan Kincaid?" she scoffed. "That's hardly likely. No, I've made up my mind, grandpa. Next year I want to be on an entirely different circuit as far from him and everyone else as we can get."

"Well, if you've decided and you feel that strongly about it, you can consider it done." He gave her shoulders a gentle squeeze. "Now, pour me a cup of coffee."

75

She hadn't expected his capitulation to be that easy. Smiling, she realized that she had forgotten how very understanding her grandfather was.

"You don't mind, do you, grandpa?" She blinked at the tears gathering in her eyes. "I know you have a lot of friends on this circuit."

"I'll make a lot more on another one," he said, winking at her. "Should I toss a coin to see whether we'll go north, east or west?"

Wrinkling her nose at him, she smiled and brushed an affectionate kiss on his leathered cheek. "I love you, grandpa. I don't care which way we go. You choose."

CHAPTER FOUR

"How's Liberty?" Patty asked, tying her hair back with a scarf as she studied the six white horses lined up in pairs.

"The swelling's gone down," Everett King answered. "I couldn't feel any heat in his legs, but I'd take it easy. Get them accustomed to the new arena and loosen them up some, then we'll see."

"Right," she nodded.

Wiping the perspiration from her palms onto the faded denim Levi's, Patty walked to the right rear horse and agilely vaulted onto his bare back. Stroking Loyalty's neck, she waited patiently while her grandfather made certain none of the reins were tangled before he handed them to her. With her grandfather walking at Liberty's head, they made their way to the arena.

The horses snorted and bobbed their heads at the newness of their surroundings as Patty guided them around the arena at a walk. As their interest reverted back to her, she stood on Loyalty's back, shifting one foot to Landmark when she had achieved her balance. Taking a wrap of the reins, she urged them into a canter, weaving them snakelike through the center of the arena, their friskiness leaving as they settled down to work.

Only once during the practice sessions did Patty take the horses through the routine she used for the performance. Constant repetition tended to make the horses anticipate each move before she gave them the signal. That anticipation would lessen her control in the event of a problem, minor or major. She slowed them to a halt at the arena gate where her grandfather stood.

"What do you think?" she asked, glancing from the tossing heads to him.

The expectant look on her face faded as she saw she had acquired an audience. Standing beside her grandfather were Morgan Kincaid, an attractive blonde in a cranberry red pantsuit, and a slender man with glasses and camera equipment hanging around his neck. Hiding her resentment at their intrusion on her private practice session, Patty nodded politely to the two strangers who were obviously from the local newspaper.

"Liberty doesn't seem to be favoring his legs.

Shall we try a jump, grandpa?" she asked.

He didn't immediately reply as he climbed over the fence and walked over to run an examining hand down Liberty's legs. After an affectionate slap on the horse's rump, the lean wiry man made his way to Patty.

"We'll make it a small one, two and a half feet. I don't want to put any strain on him, not with the performance tonight," he stated, and Patty nodded agreement. Looking past her, Everett King called out, "Morgan, will you give me a hand setting up the jump?"

When Morgan excused himself to help her grandfather, Patty noticed the way the blonde watched him swing effortlessly over the fence into the arena. She had been exposed to that animated look before. It often occurred when a woman came in contact with the aura of virility that surrounded Morgan.

As Patty moved the horses out at a walk, she wondered why so many women found his male charm so exciting when she was repulsed by it. Repulsed was probably not the right word, she decided. Perhaps her love for Lije made her immune to his attraction, or perhaps it was just that the animosity between them was too strong.

The jump was set. Instead of walking to the gate, her grandfather and Morgan moved to the center of the arena. *There must be something about Morgan to like*, Patty thought, as the now trotting horses approached the side of the two men, otherwise her grandfather wouldn't regard him as highly as he did.

Liberty stumbled slightly and Everett King immediately waved her to the center of the ring. Again the experimental hand was run knowingly down the horse's leg while the other horses moved restively.

"Maybe you should shift him to the wheel position," Morgan suggested quietly. "He's been about a step behind his partner all the time."

"Liberty has always been slower," Patty defended the horse quickly. "That's one of the reasons why we put him in the lead pair, to steady the others."

Except for a thoughtful look, Morgan ignored her comment. Her grandfather moved away from the white horse, nodding his approval without glancing at Patty.

"Take 'em over," he ordered.

Moving them away from the center she urged them into a canter, narrowing their circle to avoid the jump for three times around the arena. Each time the six horses went by the small jump, their ears pricked toward it, waiting for the signal that would take them over. Only when

Patty was satisfied with the even rhythm of their gait did she widen their circle to put them in the path of the jump.

Checking Landmark's increase in stride as they neared the white rails, Patty noticed the high arch to Liberty's head. While his lead partner gathered himself for the jump, Liberty hesitated for an instant, on the point of refusal before he hurdled the jump. That hesitation threw the others off in their stride.

Patty's heart was in her throat, waiting any second for the fall of one or more of the horses. She had to shift both feet onto Loyalty's back when Landmark fell a neck behind. The small height of the jump was the rescuer as all the horses made the jump cleanly with the exception of Liberty, who clipped the top.

Her knees were trembling badly as she continued the six horses on their circle around the track, ignoring her grandfather's voice when he called her in. Twice around she went, settling the horses into a steady canter and waiting for her legs to stop shaking beneath her. Then she widened their circle to include the jump again, certain in her own mind that Liberty's easy stride indicated he was not hurt.

The pricked ears signaled the nearness of the jump. Her voice urged the first two horses over. This time Liberty did not hold back, but leaped into the air in perfect precision with his teammate Lodestar. Not until they had made an almost complete circle of the track after the jump did Patty draw a breath of relief and turn the horses toward the stern countenance of her grandfather.

"I nearly found out what the arena tasted like on that first one!" Her laugh was shaky with the closeness of her call.

"That was a damned foolish stunt!" Morgan snapped, eyes the color of cutting blue diamonds glaring at her from the harsh ruggedness of his face.

"If Liberty had hung back the second time, I would have turned them away from the jump," Patty retorted sharply. "If I'd let him get by with it this morning, he might have tried to refuse tonight. On a bigger jump you know he wouldn't have been able to clear it at the last minute like he did this one."

"Your grandfather didn't think so. He called you in — or didn't you hear him?" Morgan already knew she had, but he was deliberately baiting her.

Patty glanced at her grandfather, who was virtually ignoring the sharp exchange as he examined Liberty again. She slipped astride Landmark an instant after Morgan had walked to his head, a steadying hand closing over the bridle.

"Yes, I heard him." Seething temper trembled her words. "But my judgment of the situation told me to take them over the jump again."

"Well, someone ought to take you over a knee!" Morgan lashed back, a black fury raging in his harsh expression.

Her hands moved to her hips in challenge. "I bet you'd like to be that someone, wouldn't you? Well, you just try it, Morgan Kincaid!"

Without warning, he reached up and grabbed her arm, yanking her off the horse's back. Patty fell against his hard chest, but he made no attempt to check her, letting her momentum take her where it would.

"You pint-sized little devil!" he growled as she recovered and pulled away from the burning contact. "Don't tempt me!"

"Why don't you take care of your stupid bucking horses and quit sticking your nose into things that are none of your concern!" she flashed angrily.

The sharply working muscles in his clenched jaw warned Patty of the tight curb he had on his temper. "I don't know whether it matters to you or not, but that stupid stunt of yours added ten years to your grandfather's age. The next time you decide to play the courageous Annie

Oakley," his lip curled with sarcasm, "give a thought to him."

The flame of her anger flickered at his sobering observation, lessening her belligerent stance. Squaring her shoulders, she returned his steel-hard gaze.

"Grandpa knows I don't take unnecessary chances," Patty replied.

"But you do put my heart in my throat once in a while," her grandfather inserted, walking to Lodestar's head. "Now, if you two don't mind, I'd like to get these horses back to the stables. And that reporter of yours might be getting impatient, Morgan."

The broad chest rose and fell as Morgan took a deep, calming breath. "Carla wants to interview you," he told Patty, "and get some pictures of you with the horses."

"Carla?" Patty haughtily raised a brow. "On first names already? My, but you do work fast!"

His gaze narrowed on her for a split second before focusing on the two spectators at the arena gate. He waved at them to enter the arena while Patty walked to Landmark's head, using the time to smother the last of the anger. She managed to smile quite naturally when Morgan introduced her to Carla Nicholson, the feature writer, and the photographer Fred Kowalski.

"What beautiful animals," the woman reporter murmured. "Sure a pure white, and so graceful and spirited." She flashed Patty a professional smile, leaving Patty with a terribly unsophisticated feeling. "I do hope their names match their beauty."

"The front pair are Liberty and Lodestar," Patty recited. "The middle ones are Legend and Legacy and the wheel horses are Landmark and Loyalty."

"Alliterative and imaginative names. That's a nice touch. Fred, get some photos of Miss King with the horses."

When the photographs were taken, her grandfather led the horses from the arena. Patty remained, patiently answering all the questions that had been put to her before at one time or another. Despite the way the attractive woman centered her attention on Patty, there was the sensation that she was attempting to impress Morgan that she was very good at her work.

"Considering how well trained your horses are, how do you feel toward the other horses in the rodeo, specifically the bucking horses?" Carla Nicholson inquired.

That question had never been asked Patty before, but she replied readily. "If you're asking if I have any favorites, the answer is yes," she smiled. "Red River."

The blonde leafed back through the pages of

her notebook. "I believe Morgan mentioned that horse, didn't you?" she glanced quickly at him.

"Yes," he nodded. "He's been bucking horse of the year a few times. This will be his last season on the circuit."

"I remember." A smile warmer than any she had given Patty spread across the woman's face as she looked at Morgan. "You told me you were going to be retiring him this year. I wanted to look at some of your stock. Would you mind, Miss King, if we walked to the pens now?"

"Of course not," Patty answered.

She half expected the woman to fall into step beside Morgan, but he and the photographer led the way while Carla Nicholson continued her questions.

"I'm curious why this particular horse is your favorite, Miss King."

"He's something of a ladies' man, I guess," Patty explained. "He's very affectionate whenever there's a woman around, although he still won't let them ride him."

"Do you know how he got his name?"

Morgan answered, "My father kept hearing about this rancher in the Red River Valley of Texas who had a horse nobody had been able to ride. He went to see him, got bucked off, and bought the horse. Originally he was named Star. After the first year on the rodeo circuit, he was referred to so often as the horse from the Red River that my father changed his name."

When they arrived at the enclosure containing the bareback stock, Morgan whistled and a golden chestnut separated itself from the other horses, trotting close to the rails and stopping to toss his head at the man who had called him. Not until Patty climbed onto the rail did the chestnut horse with the white star on his forehead come closer to butt his head affectionately against her leg, muscular and sleek, moving lightly on his feet. The gray white hairs around his nose were the single outward indication to reveal the weight of his twenty-one years.

The blonde reporter remained on the ground on the opposite side of the fence from the horse, admiring him through the slatted rails.

"I assure you he's quite friendly," Morgan promised, a warm smile softening his face. "Come on, I'll give you a hand onto the fence so that you can get a good look at him."

Patty thought that winning smile was grating and unnecessary. Carla Nicholson was already under his spell. Although she pretended an interest in the horse, she saw the provocative look the blonde reporter gave Morgan when she was perched on the fence beside him.

Neither the cranberry red pantsuit nor the pair of sandal-heeled shoes were the attire Patty would have chosen to tiptoe through the rodeo grounds. She wondered in passing if her inability to actively like the woman was because her fairness reminded her of Lije's wife.

The mocking glint in the look Morgan gave her sent a creeping heat into her face. She had the uncomfortable feeling that he was reading her mind again.

"He is a beautiful horse," Carla Nicholson was saying. "It's a pity an animal like that has to earn his keep by bucking in a rodeo. It must be a rough life for him."

There was an immediate chuckle from Morgan. "If human can come back to life in animal form, I would certainly choose to be a bucking horse! So far this year, Red has come out of the chute fifteen times. Five of those times he was ridden to the eight-second limit. This year he will actually work only four minutes and in return, he's fed, watered, sheltered and cared for as if he were a prize thoroughbred racehorse. If that's a rough life, I'll take it any time!"

"But surely those four minutes are painful, with that strap tied around his middle to make him buck?" the photographer questioned.

Morgan exchanged an amused smile with Patty before he turned slightly on the rail to call to one of the cowboys standing not too far from them.

"Kirby, bring me a flank strap." Then his attention was back to the two rodeo novices. "The hue and cry that's raised every so often at the apparent cruelty of the rodeo producers to get animals — horses and bucking bulls — to perform the way they want them to is caused by the fact that a little knowledge is dangerous because it leads to inaccurate conclusions."

Directing the two newspaper people's attention to the horse docilely nuzzling Patty's hand, he continued, "If you put an ordinary saddle on Red or any horse in the string, he would buck the average rider off every time. It's his nature. He's discovered he can get rid of the rider and be his own boss, so he'll do it every time he can for the sheer fun of it."

The flank strap was handed to Morgan by the cowboy who had fetched it. Morgan, in turn, handed it to Carla Nicholson and the photographer for their inspection.

"In rodeos, the flank strap is used to get the best performance out of the horse. It's fastened around his belly, back by the horse's hindquarters. Just like a saddle cinch, it can't be fastened too tight or it will interfere with a horse's movement. If that happens, chances are he'll simply stand in one spot and wait until you loosen it." Morgan turned the strap up so they could examine the area that actually touched the horse's belly. "This wool padding on the underside is partially for the horse's protection. But its main function is to tickle the horse's belly. Essentially what happens is that a horse will kick out with his hind feet, trying to stretch away from the object that's tickling him, exactly as a human would do. The result is that he becomes harder to ride, even for a professional rodeo rider."

"You mentioned that Red River came from a ranch. Is that where you find the majority of the rodeo stock?" Carla Nicholson asked.

"For the most part," Morgan agreed. "Dependable bucking horses are a rare commodity and a good one is expensive. That wild stubborn streak is generally being bred out of today's horses to make tractable mounts."

"Do the people contact you and tell you that they have a horse that bucks?"

"Either that, or when a rodeo is in town, the owner brings the horse in for the stock contractor to try out."

"Have you ever competed in any of the events?" Carla asked.

"When I was younger and more foolish," he

replied with a wide, mocking grin.

"What about you, Miss King?" Carla turned to Patty. "You're a good rider. Have you ever given any serious thought to riding a bucking horse? Or trying to, at least?"

"Sure I have, dozens of times," she shrugged. "Strictly as a lark, just to see if I could do it, but I wouldn't ever consider trying it professionally. I find enough thrills and risks in my own act."

"Are those the bulls in that far pen?" the photographer asked.

"That's right. Would you like to see them now?" Morgan asked, and received an immediate endorsement from both of them at his suggestion.

"I'd better go and help Gramps with the horses," Patty said, sliding easily from the top rail to the ground.

The photographer kept a protective hand on his cameras as he swung down. A vaguely helpless look crossed the blonde's face as she still sat on top of the fence rail. In the next instant Morgan, who had been the first to climb down, was reaching up, his large hands closing around her waist and lifting her safely down. Patty had the distinct impression that the feminine maneuver had been deliberate to arouse Morgan's response. She had to conceal her dislike for such trickery as the woman reporter turned to her.

"I want to thank you for your time, Miss King." Carla Nicholson offered Patty her hand, and manners dictated that she should take it. "You have a very interesting and exciting life."

To a stranger, Patty decided it might look like that, but those weren't the adjectives she would have used. The grind of constant travel, practice and almost nightly performances had become monotonous. Perhaps her outlook had become tarnished since Lije had married.

"It was my pleasure, Miss Nicholson," she nodded politely. "I know you'll find the rest of the tour just as interesting. Now I really must go."

"Wait!"

The clipped command was accompanied by a halting hand on her wrist, the hold ostensibly casual, but Patty could feel Morgan's fingers biting into the bone. Without a word of explanation, his gaze swiveled to the grizzled cowboy walking by with his arm in a cast.

"Lefty, would you step over here, please?" The battered-looking cowboy complied while Patty tried furtively to pull free of the punishing grip, without success. "I would like you to meet Carla Nicholson and Fred Kowalski from the local paper. This is Lefty Robbins, a permanent fixture on the rodeo circuit." When the introductions were out of the way, Morgan turned to the blonde. "Would you mind, Carla, if Lefty took you to the bull pens? I want to have a few words with Patty before I join you."

"Of course not." A curious glance slid to Patty's less than pleased countenance, as the blonde nodded her agreement.

As soon as the new trio were several yards away, Patty no longer tried to conceal her efforts to twist free of his hand.

"I don't know what you have to say to me," she said in a low, angry voice, "but you don't need to cut the circulation off in my hand to say it!"

The grip slackened to allow the blood to pound in her fingers again, but he didn't release her. The mask of politeness vanished with the disappearance of the newspaper people as Morgan turned the harshness of his gaze on Patty.

"I want to clear up this nonsense about you riding any bucking stock!" he snapped.

"Nonsense?" Patty frowned in startled anger.

"Yes, nonsense!" Morgan affirmed, an intimidating hardness to the set of his jaw. "You can get that ridiculous notion out of your head, because you are not climbing aboard any saddle bronc."

"Don't give me orders, Morgan Kincaid," she warned. "You're not my keeper."

"I'll give you any damned order I please and you'll obey it!"

He towered above her, black hair springing from beneath his hat while his brows were drawn together in a solid, threatening black line.

"Don't count on it," she hissed in return. "If I decide that I want to ride a bucking horse, you're not going to be able to stop me from doing it, Morgan!"

"Oh, Annie Oakley, do you have a surprise in store for you!" Morgan breathed in deeply to control his temper, blue eyes glittering with complacent triumph. "That rodeo stock in those pens belongs to the Kincaid Rodeo Company. No amateur is going to get on board any of them. They're restricted to card-carrying professional riders."

"I'm hardly an amateur!" protested Patty vigorously, refusing to give in though his point had been made. "I can ride as well as any man on this circuit!"

"Maybe you can, but you're not going to break your foolish neck while I'm around."

"Maybe?" Her voice squeaked in indignant anger. "Did you say 'maybe I can'?" Her free hand struck a defiant pose on her hip.

"Listen, you pint-sized little witch," Morgan growled. "I'm not going to argue over every word with you! I don't care if you can ride every animal in the string. I am not going to give you permission to try! Have you got that?"

"You've made your point. Now, let me go!" she demanded as she glowered at the unrelenting expression on his face.

"Not until I have your word."

"You can go to —" The rest of her sentence was lost in an outcry of pain as he sharply twisted her wrist behind her back, forcing her against the granite wall of his chest.

"Your word, Patty," he repeated.

"You're a bully and a brute. Do you know that?" She gasped at the shooting pains that were still traveling up her arm.

The nearness of his uncompromising face was unnerving, nearly as disturbing as the firm outline of his body pressed against hers.

His gaze narrowed on her trembling mouth. "I swear there's only one way to stop your insults!" he muttered savagely.

Her head was already tilted back to glare into his face. The fingers that twined punishingly into her hair jerked it back even farther. Patty's brown eyes widened; she knew that masculine mouth was about to capture hers and realized that she had not the strength to prevent it. Her pulse accelerated its pace to pound in her ears as a betraying weakness flowed into her legs.

"Hey, Morgan! Do you need any help?"

The amused laughter from a pair of onlooking rodeo hands stopped the slow descent of Morgan's mouth. It also brought a surge of renewed strength to Patty's limbs as she struggled wildly against his hold.

"Your grandfather must be the only one who has the patience to deal with you," he declared, swearing beneath his breath.

Blatantly disregarding her flailing arms and kicking feet, he picked her up and slung her over his shoulder. The blood rushed with throbbing intensity to her head as she beat at his back with her fists.

"Put me down! Do you hear? Put me down!" Her strident demands were ignored, her face flaming with the combination of blood and furious embarrassment because of the loud laughter from their audience.

His long strides began eating up the distance to the stable area; he was carrying her effortlessly. Patty tried pushing herself upright, but the grip on her thighs merely tightened.

"Put me down!" she echoed her previous demand, this time in a lower voice.

"You'd better shut up," Morgan replied with biting softness. "You're in an excellent position to be spanked, and I can't say that the thought doesn't appeal to me."

"You're an insufferable, arrogant cad!" Patty muttered, but her struggles to be free subsided at his threat. "If that blonde Carla Nicholson knew what you were really like, she wouldn't think you were nearly so attractive."

"She doesn't act like an irresponsible child either." There was an underlying thread of dry amusement in his voice.

Meaning I do, Patty thought angrily.

"What in the world —!" came her grandfather's exclamation.

Her somewhat limited view, restricted mainly to the ground beneath Morgan's feet, unless she turned her head to the side, had not told Patty how near they were to the stables where her horses were quartered.

Gasping in outrage, she found herself being unceremoniously dumped onto a bale of hay.

"Here's your granddaughter, Everett," Morgan stated, hands on his hips as he surveyed her attempts to maneuver into a less ignominious position. "Maybe you can attempt to talk some sense into her."

Her grandfather's mouth opened, the question silently written in his curious and confused eyes about to be spoken, but Morgan had abruptly turned and walked away, leaving

97

Patty to supply the answer.

"What was all that about?" Everett King inquired with a confused laugh.

"Oh, Morgan was being his usual obnoxious self, throwing his weight around – or my weight, in this case," Patty answered grimly, brushing the hay stalks from her jeans.

"What set him off this time?"

She let her gaze bounce to her grandfather's face and ricochet back to her clothes. "I told that reporter that I'd thought about riding a bucking horse. I never said I planned to do it – I only thought about it. But he had to play the dictator and tell me I couldn't do it."

"I certainly hope you don't." Everett King shook his head at the dubious wisdom of the thought.

"Don't you start in on me, grandpa!" she warned, and started toward the tack room to soap down the leather.

CHAPTER FIVE

The black rein was not lying very smoothly on Loyalty's neck. Patty slid from his back to adjust it, her trembling fingers nearly competing with her quaking knees. They had given two performances at this particular rodeo and neither had been up to her usual standards of near-flawless execution.

A pair of hands closed over her shoulders and she jumped in surprise. "Hello, Princess, I'm back," Jack Evans greeted her in a soft voice.

The kiss he attempted to brush along her neck was eluded as Patty turned around to face him, striving for a nonchalance that her stomach was far from feeling. Her glance took in the calf roper still working in the arena, the last event before her performance.

"Hi, Jack. How did you do tonight?" she asked, trying to sound lighthearted.

"I'm going to be taking the average," he winked with a boastful gleam in his eyes. "And all because of my good-luck princess. We'll have to go out tonight to celebrate."

"I don't know, Jack," Patty hedged, liking this cocky cowboy without really trusting him.

"Sure you do." He curled a finger under her chin. "We're a team. I'll meet you at the stables when the rodeo is over. In the meantime, let me give you back some of the luck you've given me."

The warmness of his lips was comforting, almost reassuring, and Patty responded in gratitude. She refused consciously to admit it, but there was an inner feeling that she would need all the luck she could get before the night was over.

"Say," Jack sighed, raising his head and studying her through narrowed eyes with a little more interest. "I'm going to have to keep my eye on you. You've been getting in a little more practice on the side, haven't you? I'm the one who's supposed to be teaching you about kissing."

"Don't be silly. Who would I practise with?" Her gaze sought the arena again as the announcer introduced the last contestant in the calf-roping event.

For the first time she noticed Morgan Kincaid leaning against the inside rails of the arena near the gate. He wasn't looking in her direction, but Patty flushed anyway.

"I'm in next," she said, checking the rein again to be sure it was lying straight, and swung herself onto Loyalty's back.

"I'll be rooting for you from the chutes," Jack promised, and patted her knee lightly before sauntering off in that direction.

Her mouth began to get dry as she watched the arena being cleared of horses and riders. She glanced at her grandfather standing at Liberty's head. He gave her a thumbs-up sign and she nodded with a weak smile.

The leader of the small four-piece band looked at her from the announcer's stand, nodding as he raised his baton. Standing up on Loyalty's back and shifting a foot to Landmark, Patty nodded to Lefty to open the gate. As it swung open, the first rousing note of "She'll be Comin' Round the Mountain" was sounded by the band.

The six white horses pranced through the gate, breaking into a spirited, rolling canter while Patty waved to the crowd, who applauded her entrance. Then every sight and every sound was blocked out as she concentrated on the routine.

The weaves, the figure eights, all were executed without error. Patty was breathing easier as she saw her grandfather supervising the erection of the jumps. She paid little atten-

101

tion to the men setting them until she sensed that something wasn't as it was supposed to be. As she circled on the inside of the arena, it took her nearly a full turn to realize that the height of the jumps was less than usual. Her lips tightened grimly as she guessed that the tall dark man standing near her grandfather was the culprit.

She reined the horses to a stop beside them. "What's going on here?" she demanded. "Those are supposed to be three-foot jumps."

"We thought it would be safer to lower them," Morgan answered.

"*We?*" Patty mocked harshly. "You mean *you* thought it would be safer. Well, you can just go and raise them to three feet. I take my horses over three-foot jumps, not kindergarten hurdles!"

"Liberty refused the second jump twice last night," her grandfather reminded her. "Both times you were able to avoid disaster by the skin of your teeth."

"But he took the jump," she added forcefully.

"Patty, you're making a scene," Morgan spoke quietly and patiently. "Take the horses over the jumps and we'll argue about it when the performance is over."

"That's what you'd like me to do, isn't it?" she turned on him, placing both feet on Land-

102

mark's back to be closer to the resolute figure. "Why don't you tell me about your plans before the performance instead of now? This is just another one of your attempts to trick me into a position where I have to do what you want. It's not going to work this time."

Morgan sighed and shook his head. "All indications are that Liberty is sound. But he still could be sore. Whatever the cause he seems to have lost his confidence. What does it matter if you have to take smaller jumps for a few nights as long as you don't injure yourself or the horses? He's one of the leaders. He has to have confidence."

Her temper wouldn't allow her to acknowledge the logic of his politely spoken argument. In a trembling rage, she jumped to the ground.

"Either you're going to raise those jumps or I am!" she declared.

She watched her grandfather and Morgan exchange glances. The slender shoulders of her grandfather lifted in a resigned shrug. Tight-lipped, Morgan turned from her and with angry, springing strides walked to the jumps and raised the bars to their customary notches.

As Patty remounted Landmark, she heard the rodeo announcer explain the delay to the audience. "Ladies and gentlemen, there seems to have been an error in the height of the jumps.

103

Miss King is having them raised."

Scattered applause followed his statement, but Patty ignored it, setting the horses at a canter and waiting for that moment when their strides settled to a rhythmic pace. Then she turned them to the jumps. Her soft voice talked to the horses, calming and urging, as the first hurdle was approached.

Liberty's ears swiveled to the jump, his neck arching a fraction in protest. The momentum of the other horses and the guiding rein carried him to it. Patty's heart screamed as she heard the solid whack of Liberty's leg against the bar, but he cleared it without mishap, stumbling only slightly as he landed before regaining his matching stride with Lodestar.

Around the arena curve, the six horses galloped slowly, the double set of jumps coming into their path. Moistening her dry lips, Patty clicked to the rhythmically bobbing heads. The bars suddenly seemed much higher and the stunt more formidable than ever before.

Closer and closer they came to the first of the obstacles until they were directly on it. As Lodestar gathered himself for the jump, Liberty tossed his head in the air and tried to turn away from the rails. His refusal had been left too late. There was no room to swing away from the jump. While Lodestar leaped into the air, Legend crowded the white horse from the rear. Valiantly Liberty tried to take the jump. His front legs cleared it, but his hindquarters caught it squarely, tumbling him to the ground.

In agonizing slow motion, Patty saw the second pair of horses attempt and fail to avoid the fallen white steed. Lodestar, unable to continue without his partner, was nearly pushed to the ground by the momentum of the second pair tumbling clumsily over the jump.

The bars were down as Landmark and Loyalty joined them, their hooves tripping on the wooden rails. Patty had already shifted her weight to Landmark's back as Loyalty lurched forward and fell into the two horses struggling to regain their footing.

In the next instant she was flying through the air as Landmark went to his knees. Instinct had not allowed her to act swiftly enough to push herself to the outside. Instead she fell between the horses. Pain screamed through her at the concussion of the arena floor. With tightly closed eyes, she waited for the moment when a flailing leg would strike her or the warm white bodies that surrounded her would roll on top.

By some miracle neither happened. Except for a few brushing blows, she lay on the sand-clay arena unscathed. Human voices wavered through the whirling chaos of her mind, the searing pain in her chest nearly separating her from reality. The oppressive heat of the horses' bodies was no longer pressing around her. The touch of a pair of hands forced her lashes to flutter open.

"Don't move!" The snapped order was issued through clenched teeth.

The blazing fire that flamed with blue lights into her face halted the hysterical impulse to laugh. Movement seemed such an impossible thing, but the order had the reverse effect of encouraging her to move, to make certain she was in one piece. Even as her lungs burned in an attempt to fill with air, Patty guessed her true motivation was to show Morgan Kincaid that she couldn't be ordered around.

When she tried to push herself into a sitting position, he roughly forced her down, little gentleness in the fingers that were probing her arms and legs for injury.

"I'm . . . a-all right," she gasped painful swallows of oxygen. "The w-wind . . . the wind w-was just knocked . . . out of m-me."

"You lie down or I'll break your neck!" The savage bite of his voice was reinforced by the black fury of his expression. "I told you, you half-witted little idiot, not to take those jumps at that height, but you knew it all! You just had to show me what an expert you were! Do you feel very expert now?" he jeered.

The last thing that Patty wanted was a flurry of I-told-you-so's, however accurate the observation. Acid tears burned her eyes as she averted her head from his harshly accusing gaze. Her grandfather was kneeling down beside her, his weathered face lined with concern, fear lurking in the recesses of his eyes.

"Patty, gal, are you all right?" Everett King murmured in a throbbing voice.

Choked, she could only nod that she was, as a tear spilled from one eye to race across a dirt-smeared cheek.

"The wind was knocked out of her," Morgan clipped the ends of the words. "I ought to break one of her arms or legs just on general principle."

"Help me up, grandpa," Patty requested tightly, hating and loathing the man who continued to taunt her with her foolishness.

But it was Morgan's arm that curved around her back, his fingers biting into her waist as he lifted her onto her feet. Her mind had already registered the fact that she was not seriously injured, but Patty felt like one big throbbing ache. Her legs were shaking badly and as much as she wanted to shake away Morgan's supporting arm, she needed it. The arena thundered with applause.

"Put me back on the horses," she said between gulping breaths as strength began flowing to her limbs again.

"Turn off the heroics, Patty!" Morgan snapped, giving her a sharp shake as if to instill some sense in her. "Besides, which injured horse would you ride?"

With a jerk of her head, Patty focused her gaze on the six white horses. She shut her eyes tightly at the sight of the blood red gash on Liberty's flank and Landmark, who was favoring his right front leg. There were cowboys at each horse's head, soothing the frightened, nervous horses while others worked swiftly to untangle the mess of harness and reins.

"How bad –" Patty could get no more out than that before an enormous lump blocked her throat.

"Nothing looks broken," her grandfather answered, touching her shoulder in reassurance.

"Oh, grandpa, I'm sorry," Patty gulped, tears running more freely through her tightly closed eyes.

"I know, honey," he replied.

"It's too late for tears now. The damage is done." Compassion was noticeably absent in Morgan's rough tone. "Wave to the crowd so we can get out of here!"

Squaring her shoulders, Patty shrugged away

from his arm, stepping free to lift an arm in salute to the cheering audience. The horses were already being led toward the gate as she turned toward it. With the same determination, she pushed her guilty feelings to the side as she tried to assess from a distance how extensive were the injuries to the horses. Lodestar was walking easily, as were Legend and Legacy. Patty tried desperately to ignore the eyes that were boring holes in her back.

"Where do you think you're going?" Morgan demanded when Patty turned with her grandfather to follow the horses to the stable area.

"To take care of the horses, of course." There was a faintly defiant tilt to her head.

Her grandfather's hand touched her arm, almost regretfully. "You'd better go to the trailer, Patty. Change your clothes. Maybe fix a cup of tea to soothe your nerves."

At her grandfather's words of agreement, Patty had stopped, turning her resentful expression on the forbidding dark features belonging to Morgan.

"I suppose that's what you think I should do, too," she challenged coldly.

"Yes, I do." But Morgan didn't leave it at that. "Just as I thought you should lower the jumps."

There was a sharp intake of breath as his

quietly spoken comment struck its mark with penetrating sureness. Pain flashed through her eyes as she tried to decipher the unreadable expression behind his sooty veil of lashes. Without any attempt to argue, Patty spun on her heel and commanded her watery legs to take her to the trailer. Perhaps she deserved that, she didn't know, but it hurt all the same.

When she stepped out of the shower more than a quarter of an hour later, the teakettle was whistling merrily on the stove. While the tea steeped, Patty dressed, donning a pair of slacks and a white knit top.

The hot cup of tea sat on the small table, her elbows on either side, her face buried in her hands. The beginning of a headache was pounding at her temples. After the first tentative sip at the fragrant liquid, Patty knew she couldn't sit idly in the trailer. She had to go to the stables and help. She couldn't leave the entire burden to her grandfather. After all, it was her fault that the incident had occurred in the first place, as much as she wanted to blame Morgan and his autocratic ways.

Leaving the tea half-drunk, Patty rose from the table, ignoring the bruises that just beginning to make themselves known. With hurried steps, she traveled the distance from the trailer to the stables, not stopping until she was pausing at the door to Liberty's stall. The top partition of the door was open and her fingers closed over the edge of the lower door.

A local vet was examining the gash on the white flank, obviously caused by one of the other horses as it fell. Patty's heart constricted painfully at the unsightly mark on the shimmering white coat.

"Is it serious?" The question came out in a taut whisper, not carrying to the vet or her grandfather standing at Liberty's head.

"Not as serious as it looks," Morgan's low voice sounded beside her, turning Patty's head with a jerk.

An unrestrainable feeling of guilt widened her brown eyes. "I — I couldn't stay at the trailer."

Diamond eyes returned her look, the ultimately masculine face self-contained and implacable. An odd tension took hold of Patty, tripping her pulse.

"So you came here," Morgan observed. "To help?"

"Yes," she nodded weakly.

Pointedly he glanced at the faint tremor vibrating her clenched fingers on the stall door. "With those shaking hands? We just got the horses settled down. The last thing they need is to be exposed to your bundle of nerves."

111

Her knuckles turned whiter as she tightened her hold, the quiet bite of his voice nearly worse than his jeering anger of before.

"It was my fault," she acknowledged softly, averting her face from his inspection. "I should be here doing something about it."

"Everything is being handled. Your grandfather will rest easier in his mind if he knows you're at the trailer. If you'd only admit it, the shock of the fall hasn't worn off."

"I'm all right!" A desperate kind of anger coated her statement.

"Physically," Morgan agreed. "But your stiff upper lip is quivering again."

Patty felt the trembling of her chin and bit tightly into her lower lip, the ensuing pain almost a relief. Why did he have to be so perceptive?

"I — I can clean the tack — or something," she argued rigidly.

"If you're trying to assuage your guilt, you'll have plenty to do taking care of the horses over the next few weeks while they recover. In the meantime, you can spend the rest of the night thanking God that the injuries weren't any more serious than they are, and reminding yourself that if you hadn't been so damned stubborn —"

"You don't have to say 'I told you so' again!" Patty broke in sharply. "I don't need you to tell me it was my fault! If you hadn't tried to trick me — Oh, what's the use!" she ended with a throbbing catch in her voice.

She started to turn her back to him, planning to walk to the tack room and soap down the leather tack, but before she could take a single step, Morgan was swinging her off her feet into his arms.

"You're going back to the trailer." As Patty started to struggle, the metallic glare of his gaze was directed at her. "I wouldn't argue if I were you," he warned with soft harshness. "I'm still thinking that a sound lecture administered to your backside might be a good thing."

Inwardly there was an acknowledgment of defeat, although Patty held herself with rigid defiance. A quaking weakness was shuddering through her body. If it had been anyone but Morgan who held her, she would have will-ingly rested her head against that muscular chest, so broad and so strong. But to seek his comfort and support was something her stub-born pride wouldn't allow her to do, no matter how miserable she felt.

So, while she stared at the inviting expanse of chest, she kept in view the powerful line of his jaw and the firm male mouth. He had already made fun of her quivering chin. She didn't want to be subjected to his mocking laughter by sobbing, however silently, on his shoulder.

"You are neither gentle nor a gentleman," Patty accused.

"Why? Because I threatened to give you the spanking you deserved?" he mocked.

"No!" she retaliated vigorously. "Because you keep rubbing it in that it was my fault. I've already admitted that it was, but you keep wanting me to grovel. Well, I won't! I feel horrible enough."

Her eyes smarted with angry tears that she refused to shed, self-pity and guilt warring with her dislike for Morgan Kincaid.

"Maybe I feel some guilt, too," he told her coldly. "I knew something like this would happen. I shouldn't have allowed those jumps to be raised." They were at the steps of the trailer when he set her on her feet, his hands keeping a grip on her shoulders while his narrowed gaze studied her upturned face, slightly startled and surprised by his unexpected admission that he was in any way to blame. "Part of the responsibility is mine for allowing that stubborn streak of pride you possess to influence me."

In the few seconds it took Patty to adjust to this new discovery, the trailer door was opened and Morgan was shoving her roughly inside.

She found herself angered by his admission.

"If you feel that way," she turned on him roundly, her brown eyes snapping as he closed the door, "then why were you so mean? You never even once asked if I was all right! You simply threatened to break my neck!"

His hands were on his hips, accepting the challenge she was laying down. "I've come to the conclusion that that's the only way to handle you. Otherwise you're so intent on proving that you're some kind of superhuman female that you'd end up killing yourself. 'Put me back on the horses,'" he mimicked. "The minute your grandfather arrived, you insisted on trying to prove what a heroine you were."

"That's what you're supposed to do when you've been thrown or have fallen."

"Not when you're too dazed to know if you're hurt or not!"

"Well, I wasn't hurt," Patty argued.

"But you could have been!" Morgan shouted back. "You could have broken your bloody neck!"

"I know that!" Her body was trembling with the supreme effort of checking her tears. Balling her fingers into tight fists, she turned from him. "Why do you always have to pick on me?" she demanded angrily. "Why can't you ever be civil? You always have to shout and order me around and tell me all the things I'm doing wrong."

"Somebody had better," he responded shortly. "You seem incapable of seeing how idiotically you behave."

"And that's why you keep tearing me down?" Patty flashed, brown eyes snapping as she darted him a fiery look. "Calling me Skinny and kid and a pint-sized Annie Oakley? Doesn't it ever occur to you that those names might hurt?"

"I thought you had an armadillo hide to go along with your stiff upper lip," mocked Morgan harshly.

"Well, I don't!" Her hair danced around her shoulders at the vigorous shake of her head. "And I don't like the way you keep making fun of me!"

"What's your suggestion?"

But she ignored his question, pursuing the trend of her own thoughts. "Why can't you ever behave decently toward me? Instead of always mocking me and laughing at what I do, making me feel like a worm, why can't you treat me like an ordinary person? Grandpa likes you so much that it seems awful that we can't be friends."

"Frankly, the thought of having you for a friend leaves me cold."

"There you go again!" Patty cried, a despairing tremor in her shrill voice. "Slapping away any attempt I make with some cutting remark."

"Would you rather have me like Jack — flirting with you and stealing a few kisses to make you think you're desirable?" he asked with biting sarcasm.

"No!" The volatile explosion that accompanied her answer spun her around.

"Then what do you want!" Morgan demanded, the harsh steel glow locking her gaze.

"I don't know." A weary, despairing sigh released most of the violence within her, leaving her drained of all but an impatient kind of weakened fury. "I just know that I'm tired of all this baiting. I'm tired of trying to defend myself against all your insults. I'm tired! Do you hear? I'm tired!"

At the last feverish exclamation, Morgan stepped forward, his hands closing over her shoulders as an impatiently resigned expression stole over his face.

"You're getting hysterical," he said grimly. "The reaction to your accident is beginning to set in."

She tried to twist her shoulders free of his grip, a betraying wall of tears filling her eyes. "Well, I certainly don't need your shoulder to cry on."

Her weak attempt to resist was ignored as he

pulled her against the hard wall of his chest, her hands still clenched in rigid fists.

"There isn't any other shoulder around," Morgan said. "You might as well use mine."

The reluctance of his offer took away what little consolation he seemed to offer. With tightly compressed lips, Patty uncurled her fingers to push away from his waist. But his strong, muscular arms had already encircled her back, becoming steel bars that refused to let her go free.

"I don't want your pity," she insisted tautly. "I don't want anything from you."

"I'm more than aware of that," Morgan answered dryly.

His hand curled around the back of her neck, forcing her head against his chest and keeping it there when Patty attempted to draw away. The steady beat of his heart and the warm hardness of his encircling arms had an enervating effect. Although reluctantly offered, there was so much comfort in just being held in someone's arms. A surrendering sigh trembled from her lips as Patty relaxed against him, waves of tiredness sweeping over her. As if she were a child, he gently rocked her from side to side and all her animosity slowly evaporated.

"I was so frightened, Morgan," Patty acknowledged, a few tears slipping from her lashes to slide down her cheeks.

"I know, kid." There was a husky softness to his voice.

His fingers wiped the tears from one cheek and brushed the hair from her face. The soothing caress was like the rough lick of a cat's tongue.

"The best thing for you to do is climb into bed and get some rest," Morgan said quietly.

Unconsciously Patty tightened the hold around his waist, not prepared to leave the security of his embrace just yet. It was so strangely right.

"Every time I close my eyes," she murmured, "I keep seeing Liberty fall. It's like watching a stop action film, a series of still frames that makes me live it all over again."

Her eyes were closed. As the pictures flashed through her mind, there was a tiny shudder of terror that quaked through her shoulders. A finger raised her unresisting chin. In the next instant the warmth of Morgan's mouth was covering hers with lazy thoroughness. The cold fear that had embraced her heart slowly melted away.

When his head was raised from hers, she was still clinging to him, her head remained tilted back against his hand, her lips trembling slightly from the satisfying pressure of his mouth. Slowly her eyes opened and she gazed into his face.

The cerulean blue of his eyes contrasted sharply with the thick sooty lashes and the ebony blackness of his waving hair. The obstinate power was in the hard lines of his features, the straight nose and strong jaw and chin. The virility, the maleness was still there. Yet Patty felt something had changed. Perhaps it was the lack of mockery in his gaze and the absence of any cynical twist to his sensual mouth.

There was a sensation that she had capitulated to something, something that she should have guarded against. Whatever it was made her heart give a frightened leap and there was a sudden, consuming necessity to say something — anything!

"What was that?" There was a thin edge of sharpness in her voice. "A kiss to make it all better?"

"Something like that." The arms around her slowly relaxed until she was standing loosely within their circle, no longer molded against his broad, muscular form. "Go to bed and get some rest." It was an order, but one that was not nearly as abrasive as she had expected. "I'll send your grandfather up so you won't be alone."

There seemed little for Patty to do except

nod an agreement, because Morgan had already released her and was walking to the outside door. It was true. She didn't want to be alone. But it wasn't her grandfather that she wanted to be with her. As the door closed, she shook her head vigorously to escape that disturbing feeling.

CHAPTER SIX

"I'm not surprised," Patty sighed wearily, affectionately stroking the neck of her black trick horse as he tugged at the hay in his stall. "I fully expected the engagements to be broken. After all, the rodeo producers were paying for a complete equestrian act, not an average trick rider. Were they able to find someone to replace us?"

"They didn't say," her grandfather answered with a shrug. "But there are plenty of quality acts around. I'm sure they'll find someone."

"Two months without any income," she sighed again.

"I've canceled the engagements for the next three months," Everett King told her with a rueful smile. "Liberty is going to take some time healing, and even then, I'm not certain that he'll make it back to his old form. We might have to start looking for a replacement."

"A replacement?" Her brown eyes widened. "That means breaking in a new horse."

122

"That's why I figured we need at least three months. We've been talking about getting a spare horse anyway. This is the time to do it."

"But our finances? How bad is it, grandpa?"

"The vet's bill, the feed bill, boarding." It was his turn to sigh. "Let's just say that it's put a healthy dent in our emergency fund, and there's more to come."

"We'll have to go back to New Mexico, won't we?" She scuffed the toe of her boot in the hay scattered along the concrete walkway in front of the stables.

"It's more than seven hundred miles back home. Texas is a big state to cross. It would be foolish to try to trailer the horses that distance in their condition. Foolish and risky."

"But we can't afford to stay here either," Patty pointed out. "Not without any money coming into the kitty, only going out for stalls and feed."

"And to the vet," her grandfather added.

"We have to go back," she said, repeating her earlier statement only with more force and determination. "We can make the trip in stages, resting the horses for a couple of days in between."

"Do you think it's a good thing for us to go back?" he asked quietly.

"A good thing?" Patty frowned, glancing at

123

him in confusion. "Of course! It's the only thing. What do you mean?"

"I was thinking about Lije. Back at your parents' ranch, you're bound to run into him and his wife."

For a freezing second Patty couldn't reply. It was impossible! She hadn't given Lije Masters a single thought. Always before the thought of her parents' home in New Mexico had been synonymous with the thought of Lije Masters, the man who had filled her heart and mind for as long as she could remember. Now suddenly, they were separate. She couldn't believe it. How had it happened?

"Patty?" The weathered hand of her grandfather touched her arm, his voice echoing the concern in his eyes as he gazed into her nearly colorless face. "You're white as a sheet. What's wrong?"

"I . . . I . . ." Patty stumbled, unable to put into words what she couldn't understand herself.

"Is it your shoulder again?"

"Yes." She seized on his suggestion almost with relief, using the excuse of the slight shoulder strain she had suffered as a result of the fall. "I've been favoring it, I guess," she murmured.

"You're as tense as a bucking horse waiting for the chute to open." He shook his head as his experienced fingers touched the tight muscles in her neck. "Turn around here."

Patty did as she was ordered, turning her back to her grandfather while he began gently manipulating and kneading the taut cords, forcing them to relax.

"We certainly can't stay here, grandpa," she said after a few minutes, her eyes closed as she enjoyed the soothing massage.

"I don't think we should go back to the ranch."

"There isn't any place else we can go. Besides, it doesn't matter."

"I still don't think it's a good thing to go stirring up the ashes of a dead fire."

The grim determination in his voice was vigorously apparent. A dead fire – the words lingered in Patty's mind. Perhaps that was it. Perhaps she had finally got over her heartbreak. She could even visualize Lije's face without any knife blades twisting inside.

"What's the alternative, grandpa?" she asked.

His hands left her neck and shoulders for a moment. She started to turn around and they were replaced. Their touch was more firm than before, a hard strength that demanded her muscles to surrender under its pressure. A sudden tingle raced down her spine and her lashes flew open with a start.

"I've already offered the alternative."

She hadn't really needed Morgan Kincaid's voice to realize why the hands had felt so different. She jerked away and pivoted at the same time. She readily picked up the mocking challenge that was in his gaze.

"What alternative?" she demanded.

"Morgan's ranch is less than two hundred miles from here." Her grandfather answered for him. "He's offered to let us keep the horses there as long as we take care of them, until they're ready to go back on tour."

"That's your parents' ranch, isn't it?" Her head was tilted back in defiance, not liking the feeling that she was being maneuvered again. "They might not be so willing to extend their hospitality so openly."

"It's a family holding," Morgan corrected with a slow drawl, amusement flickering in his blue eyes. "Plus, I've already discussed it with dad to be certain he had enough stable room available. The invitation has been seconded, so your objections on that score are meaningless."

"Neither grandpa nor I need your charity!"

"It isn't charity. It's only a neighborly Oklahoma offer." The broad shoulders moved in an expressive shrug as if he had plainly expected her to take this stand. "I wouldn't be much of a friend if I didn't offer your granddad a helping hand when he needed it. I already warned him that I thought you would refuse."

"You're right. I do!" Patty declared.

"Well for my part, I accept," Everett King stated firmly.

"Grandpa!" Gasping his name, she turned on him with a look of surprised outrage.

"It's logical and practical and I've made up my mind." He held up his hand to halt the torrential outpouring of anger that was about to spring from his granddaughter's lips. "You can argue, shout and throw all the tantrums you want, but you aren't going to change my decision. We can't afford to stay here. It would be foolish and risky to go all that far back to New Mexico. So I'm taking the horses to Morgan's ranch and you can come or stay as you please."

"Grandpa!" Patty breathed, unable to believe that he had taken such an adamant stand against her. In the past, all major decisions had been the result of joint agreement. Even when she was a teenager he had treated her as an equal partner in a business venture. "You can't mean it?"

"The way I see it, Patty, we have no choice." There was a look of apology in his eyes, but the determination in the rest of his expression didn't waver. "Morgan's leaving in a couple of hours with the rodeo stock. The decision has to be made now so he can let them know at the ranch."

With a hopeless sense of frustration, Patty darted a glance at Morgan, silently accusing him of waiting until the last moment to extend his invitation.

"I would have suggested it earlier, but I wasn't aware there was any difficulty," he explained calmly with his usual perception of her thoughts. "When your grandfather indicated to me yesterday that you might be having some rough going, I had to wait until I'd checked with dad to be certain there was room available for you."

"We could have made it," Patty asserted.

"I've said it before," the ebony-dark head moved to the side in a despairing shake, "you are the hardest person in the world to help. You and that pride of yours keep looking for an ulterior motive where there is none. It's a straightforward offer to let you stay on the ranch until your horses recuperate and you can get back on tour."

He held her gaze for a long moment, transmitting some silent message that there was nothing for her to worry about. Yet Patty couldn't shake off the feeling that there was. She broke free of the compelling blue eyes and glanced helplessly at her grandfather.

"Will you let them know I'll be there, Morgan?" Everett King requested, not reacting to the silent plea in her eyes. "The horses should be able to travel a week from Tuesday."

"I'll tell them to look for you, then," Morgan nodded, his gaze sliding again to her. "What about you, Patty? Should I tell them to expect you, too?"

Taking a deep breath, she tried to gain time, hoping that in the precious seconds, she would come up with another solution. Of course she didn't. There didn't seem to be any other.

"Yes," she agreed, exhaling tiredly and turning away.

"Goodbye, Patty," Morgan said to halt her departure. "I won't be seeing your for a couple of months or more." His mouth quirked into a mocking smile. "It will seem like a well-earned vacation for both of us."

Staring at his hard, strong face, Patty realized she had forgotten that. Morgan wouldn't be there to torment her with his mockery and laughter. As much as she disliked him, he had become something of a fixture in her life.

"Yes, it will seem like that, won't it?" she admitted aloud.

"Who knows?" The massive shoulders shrugged with his drawling voice. "I might even discover that I'll miss you, or at the very least, I'll miss our constant arguments."

Before she could retort that she wouldn't miss him at all, he was turning to her grandfather and bidding him goodbye and the opportunity to administer one last cutting barb had passed. There was a vague tightness in her throat as she watched him walk away. The peace and quiet would be wonderful, she told herself.

"I'm sorry, Patty," her grandfather spoke at last.

For an instant, she couldn't remember why he was apologizing. "It's all right, gramps," she answered quietly. "I only wish there had been some other way we could have got by without accepting Morgan's offer."

"You still can't abide him, can you?"

"I never will!" Patty declared vehemently.

"He's a good man," Everett King pointed out, then turned toward the stalls. "I'm going to check on Landmark."

Most of the rodeo cowboys had left the day before, but when Morgan pulled out with his men and the rodeo stock, the arena grounds seemed like a deserted ghost town. Although Patty and her grandfather were kept busy caring for the injured horses, the loneliness crept in. It wasn't the hustle and bustle that she missed so much as it was an indefinable something else.

Tuesday morning, the day they were to leave, her spirits lightened considerably. She still didn't like the idea of going to Morgan's ranch. Considering the animosity she held toward him, she felt guilty accepting the hospitality of his parents.

Watching her grandfather load the last horse into the trailer, Patty stood back, trying to understand the conflicting emotions that had her looking forward to the journey and feeling guilty at the same time. The only answer that came to mind was that she was glad to escape the emptiness of the grounds, although being alone and separated from other people had never bothered her when she was growing up on her parents' ranch.

"All loaded up and ready to go," her grandfather announced as he locked the trailer gate in place.

"Do you want me to lead the way or follow?" she asked.

"You'd better follow me for a while until we see for sure how the horses are going to do. When we get to the Oklahoma border, you can take the lead."

"You go ahead and start out. I'll catch up," Patty said after nodding in agreement.

"You aren't still mad at me, are you?"

"I'm not mad at you," she frowned.

"You've been so quiet all week I thought you were upset because I'd accepted Morgan's offer. I only did what I thought was best."

"I know that, grandpa," she smiled, letting her dimples come into play. "And I couldn't be holding any grudges or I wouldn't be going along. But you knew that all the time."

"It makes me feel better to hear you say it," he smiled in return. "Now, we'd better get on the road or we'll be traveling all day."

After a jaunty salute in her direction, Everett King climbed agilely into the cab of the pickup and started the motor. Waving her own good-bye, Patty set out for her pickup and the travel trailer parked some distance away. Her grandfather was pulling out of the rodeo grounds gate as she neared hers.

Blinking uncertainly, Patty looked again toward the passenger side of her truck. There was the crown of an ivory stetson hat level with the window. Someone had evidently decided to hitch a ride. Her mouth smoothed into a firm, angry line as her long legs carried her to the passenger door.

"Get out of there!" she ordered, and yanked the door open at the same time.

There was a startled curse of pain as the man who had been leaning against the door nearly fell out, caught himself with a hand on the door, and straightened back into an upright position in the seat.

"For God's sake, you could be more careful!" Morgan Kincaid growled. "I could have broken my neck when you pulled the door open that way!"

Patty's mouth opened in surprise as she stared into his blazing blue eyes and the stern, forbidding frown beneath the wayward strands of black hair.

"What are you doing here?" she demanded when she had recovered her speech.

"I could ask you the same question," he retorted. "I thought your grandfather always drove the truck pulling the travel trailer."

"He changed this time so he could keep a closer watch on the horses," she answered instinctively, forgetting for a moment that he had not answered her question.

He turned in the seat to face her with painstaking slowness. "You could have checked to see who was in here before nearly killing them," he muttered angrily.

It was only when he had completed the turn that Patty saw his left arm was in a sling. Her anger and surprise evaporated into curiosity and concern.

"What's happened to your arm?"

"I dislocated my shoulder. And damned near did it again when you tried to send me sprawling on the ground!" Morgan retorted. "Who did you think was in here, anyway?"

"I supposed it was a hitchhiker," Patty defended herself. "How was I supposed to know it was you?" Suspicion loomed to the front. "Did grandpa know you were going to be here?"

"Of course he didn't!" Morgan snapped. "If he had I would have known which truck he was pulling now, wouldn't I?"

"Then what are you doing here?"

His mouth moved into a cold, exasperated smile. "I wanted a ride home and I knew that was where you were going." With his good hand, he lifted his slinged arm slightly. "I can't drive very well with this."

"How did it happen?" Her train of thought reverted back to his injury.

"Snowball went through the fence. I was, unfortunately, on the other side," Morgan replied tautly.

Snowball, Patty knew, was one of the rodeo bulls, renowned for his complete lack of respect for the height or thickness of any fence if he chose to be on the opposite side. He was a Brahman cross, but an extremely mild-tempered beast unless he got a notion in his mind to wander.

"What happened to Snowball?"

There was a suggestion of amusement in Morgan's blue eyes. "He's a good draw for the cowboys and always gives them a good score when they ride him. So I sold him to the Jim Byers' outfit. I figured they could borrow trouble for a while."

"How did you get here?"

"Bob Andrews' wife had a baby, a boy, and he gave me a lift as far as here."

"But what about the rodeo stock?" Patty questioned.

"Listen, if you keep asking all these questions, your grandfather is going to be thirty miles down the road. Don't you think we ought to be going?"

"Oh, yes, we should," she agreed, brought back suddenly from her curiosity to the business at hand.

Morgan slammed his door shut while Patty walked around to the driver's side. Not until she was out on the highway did she take the time to repeat her question.

"Who's in charge of the stock while you're gone?"

"My brother Alex and his wife drove down on Sunday. He's taking over while I give my shoulder a couple of weeks to heal."

"A couple of weeks?" Patty repeated uncertainly.

The sideways glance she gave him was met with a mocking gaze. "What's the matter, Skinny? Are you trying to be certain how long you're going to have to put up with me around?" Morgan taunted. "I don't know about you, but I was just beginning to enjoy the peace and quiet."

"So was I," Patty was stung to retort, refusing to admit that she had found it empty.

"Well, never fear," said Morgan, settling down in the seat and tipping his hat forward to cover his face. "You won't have to suffer my company any longer than is necessary. That should relieve your mind." He cradled the sling in his good arm. "Now, if you don't object, I'm going to take a nap. And please, drive carefully. I'm in enough pain as it is without getting my teeth jolted out of my head."

"I always drive carefully!" she snapped. "And don't take it out on me just because you're hurt!"

At that particular moment, a railroad crossing loomed in front of them. Patty's concentration had been more on her passenger than on the road and she was unable to slow up in time before they bumped across it, drawing a muffled exclamation of pain from Morgan.

"If that's an example of careful driving —" he began savagely.

"Oh, shut up!" And she reached over and switched on the radio to drown out the rest of his jeering remark. "Don't talk to me again until your disposition improves."

Morgan reached over and turned the radio down. "Your disposition doesn't exactly rate a gold star," he responded dryly, and resumed his former position, the brim of his hat concealing his angry look.

"My disposition? You've been yelling at me from the beginning!" Patty answered.

"Talking loudly," he corrected. "Now be quiet so I can get some sleep."

Pressing her lips tightly together in mutinous silence, Patty concentrated on the highway in front of her. Several miles farther on, she caught sight of the horse van her grandfather was pulling and began gaining ground until she was a hundred feet or more behind him.

Morgan too was silent, presumably asleep if the even rise and fall of his chest was anything to go by. His presence grated her nerves, never allowing her to totally relax and become oblivious to him. Forgetting how pallid the peace of last week had seemed, she found herself wishing for it.

After an hour's drive, the horse trailer in

front of her flashed its turning signal and pulled off the highway into a rest area. Patty eased her foot off the accelerator and followed, resisting the impulse to apply sudden brake pressure and rudely awaken Morgan. But the change in speed did not go unnoticed as the hat brim was pushed back and bright blue eyes looked around at the new surroundings.

"Is he having any problems up ahead?" he asked when Patty stopped the pickup and travel trailer parallel with her grandfather.

"He didn't signal that he was," she answered shortly.

The question was repeated to Everett King the instant he stepped from the cab of his truck. The genuine surprise on her grandfather's face at the sight of Morgan removed the last remaining doubt Patty had that this coincidence might have been arranged.

"No problems that I know of," her grandfather responded to the question. "Just taking a breather for the horses. What are you doing here?"

While Morgan repeated his explanation, Patty walked to the horse trailers, using her own key to unlock the access door. They had lined the van's stalls with extra padding for the journey to insure that the horses didn't accidentally do further injury to themselves. Before she could actually begin the individual inspections, her grandfather was entering the van.

"I'll check the horses," he said. "Why don't you get some cups from the trailer and pour us all some coffee? Bring a sack of cookies, too."

Breathing in deeply, Patty checked the impulse to suggest that they not stop for a break but continue on. The rest was for the horses, not themselves.

"Okay," she sighed in agreement, and walked back through the door, hopping to the ground before Morgan could take the few steps necessary to offer her a hand.

With only a freezing glance in his direction, she walked around the horse van, rummaging again through the pocket of her tight Levi's for the key to the trailer door. She was just taking the cups out of the cupboard when Morgan stepped in.

"Would you like some help?" he offered.

After the angry exchange not an hour before, Patty resented the easy way he was slipping into casual friendliness. She couldn't pretend so readily that their argument hadn't occurred.

"Aren't you afraid you'll hurt your good arm?" she asked caustically.

"I see you're still nursing your temper," Morgan commented dryly.

"What was I supposed to do? Ignore the way

you yelled and swore at me earlier? You were the one who was a grouchy old bear," Patty accused, as she searched impatiently through the shelves for the sack of cookies.

"I was, wasn't I?" His voice came from only a few feet away, paralyzing Patty for an instant because she hadn't heard his footsteps. "I owe you an apology. I suppose it was a lack of sleep, this shoulder and your less than cordial welcome. But I am sorry."

"I'm surprised you're capable of admitting that." Although her reply came out bitterly acid, there was a sudden flow of warmth through her system. "I didn't realize you could be wrong in anything."

"You still want to fight, don't you? Are you holding onto your grudge against me because your grandfather accepted the invitation to my home?" he asked quietly. "I know you probably regard it as some sort of punishment to be endured, but I assure you my parents are very warm, friendly people."

"It's a pity you don't take after them." The sack of cookies was in her hand as she turned from the cupboard, keeping her gaze averted from his face.

"You've never bothered to get to know me well enough to know whether I do or not," Morgan pointed out, his tall frame blocking the path to the door. "Let me carry that."

"You only have the use of one arm." Patty ignored his outstretched hand, setting the sack on the counter to slip the cup handles on her fingers.

"I'm hardly an invalid."

To prove his point, fingers closed over her wrist, biting in sharply to draw her to him, the cups clanging against each other at the sudden movement. Her free hand came up to push him away and encountered the sling. To apply force against his injured shoulder would secure her release, but Patty couldn't hurt him deliberately.

The virile masculine face was only inches from her own, the tantalizing firmness of his mouth within easy reach. His grip had twisted her arm behind her back, molding her against his length and quickening her pulse at the hard imprint of his male outline.

"Are you going to accept my apology or keep throwing my ill temper in my face for the rest of the trip?" Morgan asked softly.

"I accept it." Although grudgingly issued, there was a breathy catch to her voice that Patty couldn't control.

"And forgive me?" he prompted.

She darted an angry glare into his mocking blue eyes. "Yes."

Lightly he brushed his lips against hers, playing with them for a provocative second before drawing away. There was a funny ache in the pit of her stomach that wouldn't go away even when Morgan released her entirely and picked up the sack of cookies. Now that he no longer held her, Patty wanted to lash out at him in anger. A warning light must have flashed in her eyes.

"Cheer up, kid," he laughed softly. "I'll only be around for a couple of weeks. You've endured my company for a lot longer time and managed to survive."

"I am not a child!" Patty retorted.

"No, you're a stubborn baby goat. Some day you're going to get tired of butting your head against me," he agreed with a complacent nod of his head. "Now quit dawdling and get those cups out to your grandfather. He's probably waiting for his coffee."

"When we start back out, you can ride with him." The taut declaration was drawn though clenched teeth.

"And deprive myself of your friendly company? I don't think so." A satisfied smile deepened the grooves around his mouth and nose as he walked out the trailer door ahead of Patty.

CHAPTER SEVEN

Clay red soil churned in the water, changing the colorless liquid to a murky red shade. The same red soil lined the banks of the river and surfaced to form tiny island bars in the river itself. The Red River, part of the borderline between Texas and Oklahoma.

"Welcome to Oklahoma, the Sooner State," Morgan said as the pickup traversed the bridge over the Red River and onto the highway stretching northward.

"Why the Sooner State?" Patty asked with a wry curve to her mouth. "The sooner you get here, the sooner you can leave?"

"Have I ever spoken disparagingly of your home state?" he asked with a hint of reproving sharpness.

"I don't know. Have you?" she countered.

Her sliding gaze encountered his uncompromising profile. There was a slight grimace of pain as Morgan shifted his position in the seat. Patty guessed that his shoulder had to be

143

bothering him, although he had not once referred to it in the last hour's drive.

"I am curious," she said, leaving the sarcasm out of her words. "Why is it called the Sooner State?"

There was an instant of silence and she felt his measured look studying her face. There was a slight vibration of her nerve ends in response to the almost physical touch of his eyes.

"The word dates back to the land rush days. In the beginning it had an uncomplimentary connotation. The settlers who were referred to as 'Sooners' earned it by being accused of jumping the gun, you might say, and staking their claims for homestead land before it was actually open for homesteading. Often it was wrongly applied to those people who obtained choice pieces of land by others who had settled on nearly worthless ground. Poor losers, I guess," Morgan explained. "That meaning has been pushed to the background and a 'Sooner' is now simply a nickname for an Oklahoman."

"How much farther to your ranch?"

"Not far now," he answered, his gaze turning out the side window of the pickup. "We're north and west of Ardmore, near the foot of the Arbuckle Mountains. This river peninsula we're on right now used to be a refuge for outlaws. Some of them are buried here near

Thackerville. Have you been in Oklahoma before?"

"I've been through it," Patty answered non-
committally.

"Maybe you'll have a chance to see some of it
while you're here." But Patty noticed he didn't
offer his services as a guide. "The pine forests of
the Ouachita to the east are very beautiful, especially the drive through the Winding Stair Mountains. And Turner Falls in the Arbuckle
Mountains. Have you been to the National Cowboy Hall of Fame in Oklahoma City?"

'No."

"You and your grandfather will have to make
a point to go there."

"Yes," she agreed, stifling a disappointed sigh
that had come from nowhere. "Yes, I suppose
so."

A half an hour later they were turning west of
Ardmore onto a state road. After another quarter of an hour's drive or more, Morgan pointed
out the ranch road, marked simply by a sign on
a post carved with the name Kincaid. Slowing
the pickup down, Patty eased it over the open
rails of the cattle guard and followed the grav-
eled clay road into the rolling hills, trailed by
her grandfather with the horse van.

They traveled several miles into the open country before Patty sighted the main building of the

ranch protected by a small hill rising on the northwest from the cold blast of winter storms. The tall, rambling brick house with its clay red brick and cream white trim was off to the side. The white stables and barns were to the northeast of the house, accented by interlacing corrals and a small rodeo arena complete with bucking chutes and a judging stand.

As she followed the lane that made a wide circle to encompass both the house and the ranch buildings, Patty saw a tall man striding effortlessly from the nearest white barn to meet them. His height made him appear deceptively lean and well muscled, but Patty wasn't taken in. The resemblance of the man to Morgan was too strong for her not to guess that it must be his father.

When the distance lessened and his features became more discernible, Patty knew she was right. His face was strong, perhaps not nearly so unrelenting as Morgan's, and lines crinkled the corners of his eyes in a friendly way. The sideburns were snow shite, but the rest of his hair was ebony black with an occasional strand of white.

"You can park by the stock trucks near the barn," Morgan said, and Patty complied.

Morgan was out of the pickup within seconds after it had stopped, waving to her grandfather to park beside Patty. Then she watched the warm handclasp between father and son, the mockery erased from Morgan's face by a broad smile. She wanted to wait for her grandfather, but as the two men turned their attention to her, she knew she couldn't.

As she slid from the cab of the truck, a screen door slammed at the house and a woman hurried with light grace toward Morgan. Her dark auburn hair was liberally streaked with gray, but the multitude of freckles on her face made her seem eternally young. Patty waited discreetly near the door of the truck while Morgan greeted his mother.

"It's so good to see you again!" Mrs. Kincaid declared gaily as he lowered his head to receive the firm kiss she placed on his cheek. "It seems like ages. How's your shoulder?"

"Don't fuss, Molly. Morgan's barely home," the low teasing voice of the older man scolded.

"Patty, come here," Morgan motioned her over to their group. "I want you to meet my parents."

Unwillingly she obeyed, wishing he had ignored her for a few more minutes until her grandfather had positioned his trailer. Despite her initial nervousness, she found herself responding to their warm smiles of welcome.

"So this is your harum-scarum Annie Oakley,

huh, Morgan?" Lucas Kincaid laughed.

"This is the one and only," Morgan agreed, a mysterious smile flitting across his face as he met Patty's defiant look. "Thank heavens I don't think she can shoot as well as she can ride or else I would be dead by now."

"Morgan, you shouldn't exaggerate so," his mother reprimanded.

"I don't think I'm exaggerating, am I, Skinny?" Again there was that knowing look of amusement at the snapping fire in her brown eyes. "Many times she's suggested that I go to a warm place."

"And you probably deserved it, too!" Molly Kincaid retorted.

"Do you feel better now, Patty?" Morgan asked quietly, lowering his voice but not sufficiently to exclude his parents.

"What do you mean?" she asked tautly, feeling decidedly on the defensive.

"You now have an ally in the enemy camp — namely my mother. Surely you won't find your stay here nearly so objectionable," he replied.

Patty colored furiously, glancing in embarassment at the older couple. She stared in humiliating silence at the ground, wishing his parents weren't there so she could tell Morgan off.

"You don't need to hold your tongue on their account," he mocked softly. "Mom and Dad are aware of the state of war that exists between us."

"Don't tease Patty so," his mother frowned.

"Don't worry, Mom," he chuckled. "She fights back." But his attention was diverted from tormenting Patty by the arrival of her grandfather.

It was one thing to hurl insults at Morgan in private. But Patty was reluctant to do so in front of his parents and he seemed to know it and was taking advantage of it.

After Everett King had been introduced to Morgan's parents, he said, "I'd like to get the horses unloaded and settled in right away, if you don't mind."

"Of course not," Lucas Kincaid agreed readily. "I'll show you the stalls we've got ready for you."

As Patty started to follow the two older men, Molly Kincaid laid a detaining hand on her arm. "Come up to the house with me and I'll show you your rooms."

"Rooms?" Patty repeated blankly, turning toward their travel trailer to explain that she and her grandfather would be staying in it. "We —"

Morgan's hand curled under her hair to circle the back of her neck. The pressure of his touch turned her automatically away from the trailer and his mother. His gaze locked onto hers, refusing to release her.

"Would you mind if I spoke privately to Patty for a few minutes, mom?" The request was addressed to his mother although his eyes, steely blue, never left Patty's face.

"But —" Patty started to protest vigorously, but the biting pressure of his grip halted the flow.

The auburn-haired woman looked uncertainly at Patty before sending a slightly warning glance at her son. "Come up to the house when you're through."

"We will," he answered her firmly as she walked away.

"You know very well that grandpa and I are staying in our trailer," Patty declared before Morgan had a chance.

"Listen very carefully, Patricia King." His gaze narrowed on her belligerent expression. "I am not going to repeat myself. When we go up to the house, you are going to very politely accept the rooms my mother has fixed especially for you and your grandfather. You are not going to say one word to indicate in any way that you would rather reject her hospitality and remain apart. However much you dislike me, I am not going to allow you to let it reflect on my parents. Do you understand?"

Patty stared into the set features, longing to tell him to go take a flying leap off a cliff, but the intimidating line of his mouth prevented the words from getting out. In this, she realized, he was going to stand for no arguments.

"I'm not as uncivilized and cruel as you are," she retorted. "I would never take my dislike of you out on your parents, and I think it's mean of you to suggest that I would."

"I figured that your pride would rear its ugly head again," Morgan drawled. "And you can be unconsciously stubborn."

"If I am, you are the one who's given me cause to be that way," retaliated Patty.

"Don't try to change the subject."

"I wasn't! And stop ordering me around like a child. I'm not a child!" She almost stamped her foot in an infantile tantrum. To disguise the movement, she turned away, hot tears building in the back of her eyes. "If this is the way it's going to be, I wish I'd never come," she muttered bitterly.

"Where would you have gone? Back to New Mexico and Lije?" Morgan scoffed. "Were you hoping to do a little reconnaissance to see if he was as happy with his wife as he appeared?"

Pivoting sharply back, she swung her hand in a swift arc and connected with his cheek, the night's growth of dark beard scraping the palm of her hand. Morgan caught her wrist in its downward movement to prevent her from slapping again.

There was an ominous narrowing of his eyes. "What's the matter? Did I get too near the truth?"

"You couldn't have been farther from it!" Her voice trembled violently. "I don't care whether you believe me or not, but Lije Masters means nothing to me! I wish him all the happiness in the world — in his marriage and his new family!"

"Those are brave words. Too bad there isn't any ring of truth in them," he mocked.

"You couldn't see the truth if it spat in your eye! The only thing you can think about is making my life miserable. Why must you pick on me so?" Patty asked with an angry, despairing sigh.

"Somebody has to shake some sense into you."

"Does it have to be you?" It was a strange question, but one that was spoken before she had a chance to think about it.

There was a faintly inquiring tilt to his head, a lightning change from stern anger to curious amusement. "Are you tired of fighting me, Patty?"

"Yes," was the clipped admission.

"I never thought the day would come when I'd hear you say that," Morgan replied, a vaguely satisfied expression in his strong face.

"Well, you have, and you needn't be so triumphant about it," she muttered.

"Was I? I'm sorry." A warm smile was offered in accompaniment of his apology.

Her heart thudded against her rib cage as she felt his virile charm working its spell on her. A desire to be held within the strong circle of his arms rushed unchecked through her veins. The reaction of her senses to his smile struck her as being slightly mad. Briskly she averted her gaze from the captivating gleam in his eyes.

"May we go to the house now?" she requested tight-lipped.

"First I want to get one thing straight. Hear me out," Morgan inserted at her accusing glance. "I didn't know until a few minutes ago that my mother intended you and your grandfather to stay at the house. If I had, I would have mentioned it earlier, and not had her spring it on you unexpectedly. But since she has made these plans, I hope you'll accept them."

The low conciliatory tone coaxed a surrendering nod from Patty as she submitted to his quietly spoken request. "I will," she agreed.

And the undeclared truce began.

During the following five days, not one harsh word was exchanged between the two of them. Patty acknowledged that they didn't see each other that often, mainly at mealtimes or at the stables, and then generally in the company of others. Morgan still teased her, called her Skinny, but there were no disguised insults in his remarks.

As for his parents, Patty decided she could become quite fond of them. His mother, vivacious and warm, made her feel she was a member of the family. When Patty wasn't at the barns helping her grandfather take care of the horses, she was at the house helping Molly Kincaid prepare meals and clear away the dishes of the last one.

Lucas Kincaid was a big, vital man, embracing life and those he loved with an invisible bear hug. A great storyteller, he livened the dinner table with his tales, invariably spun with his droll Western humor. In appearance, he and Morgan were similar, but each personality was distinctly drawn. They were independent individuals, caring deeply for each other but not intimidated by each other's shadow.

Their home was a vision of simplicity and charm, rustic in its furnishings with casual early American furniture adding to the Western atmosphere. But Patty's discerning eye hadn't missed the implied wealth that lurked unpretentiously in the corners, the intricate bronze sculptures of Frederic Remington and his paintings depicting the lusty frontier life, and other works of art and prints by equally famous Western artists scattered about the house. But it was a place that was lived in with love and happiness, an atmosphere that could not be bought with any amount of money. It was a gift from the hearts of its occupants.

Burying her head deeper in her pillow, Patty tried to block out whatever sound it was that had awakened her. Then it came again – a whinnying neigh from the stables. Easily she distinguished the caller, one of her own white horses, Landmark. Lifting her head from the pillow, she glanced at the luminous dial of the clock on the bedside table. Nearly midnight, the hands revealed.

This was about the time her grandfather made his nightly check on the horses. He never turned in until late, declaring now that he was old, he didn't need as much sleep. Patty waited, trying to decide if the whinny had been one of welcome or a call for help. Her grandfather could be at the stables or he might have already checked on them and left. She waited, all thought of sleep gone.

After several minutes of continued silence, Patty threw back the covers and slipped out of bed, padding in her bare feet to the window. From this angle with the branches of the large oak in the way, she couldn't tell if there was a light on in the stables. She walked to the door of her downstairs bedroom and listened for the sounds of anyone stirring in the house. There was only the ticking of the large grandfather clock.

Retrieving the light cotton robe from the end of her bed, Patty slipped her arms into it to cover the bareness exposed by her shortie pajamas. With quiet movements she tiptoed from the room. Moonlight streamed in through the windows, making artificial light unnecessary as she hurried quietly to the less obstructed view from the living-room window.

The stable was dark. There were no lights shining in its small windows. With the house quiet, her grandfather must have looked in on the horses already and retired for the night. Another whinny came from the stable, muffled this time because there were no windows open as there had been in Patty's bedroom. Still, she was certain she had detected a plaintive note in the sound.

She hesitated uncertainly near the window, unable to decide whether to check on the horses herself or get her grandfather. Finally she decided on the last. Chances were he was not yet asleep and if there was a problem, she would have to seek him out anyway. Under someone's guidance, she could care for any horse's injury, but she didn't have the experience to diagnose a problem.

The closed stairwell to the upper floor was dark, the moonlight unable to peer around the corners to pierce the gloom. Her fingers touched the light switch and hesitated. Her grandfather's bedroom was the second door on the right at the top of the stairs. Patty had no wish to accidentally waken the rest of the household with what might be no more than a false alarm.

With a hand on the banister, she climbed the stairs, a board creaking occasionally as it took her weight. Her hand searched the darkness at the top of the stairs for the side wall. Several hesitant steps later, the firmness of the solid wall was touched by her fingertips. Trailing them along the wall, Patty encountered the first door, tiptoed by it and paused beside the second door.

Silence and the even sound of someone breathing greeted her as she opened the door and quietly closed it behind her. Just inside the room, she hesitated, unwilling to waken her grandfather if he was truly asleep. The limbs of another large oak blocked the flow of moonlight, admitting only enough light for her to discern the shadowy human form in the bed.

With unconscious stealth, she edged closer to the bed until she was bending over it. When the dark figure stirred her mouth opened to call out softly to him. Only a startled gasp of surprise came out as her wrist was seized and she was pulled onto the bed. The rest of her cry was smothered by the large hand that covered her mouth. Wide brown eyes gazed horror-struck into the glinting blue eyes of Morgan Kincaid only inches above her.

"I wonder what my mother would think if she found you creeping into my bedroom in the middle of the night," he laughed softly, his warm breath dancing over her skin.

The shock receded as his mocking words provoked a spurt of anger. Not only his hand but his body weight was pushing her into the mattress. She managed to push his hand away, at least as far as the side of her neck.

"What are you doing in grandpa's room?" she demanded in an accusing whisper.

"I don't think mother would buy a case of mistaken rooms," Morgan taunted, "since this has been my bedroom almost since the day I was born."

The hand she raised to push him off encountered the searing bareness of his chest, muscles rippling beneath her touch, igniting all sorts of fiery sensations that left her slightly breathless.

"This isn't grandpa's room?" Her voice sounded very weak even to her own ears. "But — but this is the second room on the right," she added lamely.

"The second room, yes." A half smile curved the inflexibly male mouth, "but the third door. You forgot about the linen closet."

A tiny oh slipped from her parted lips. She moistened them nervously and saw his gaze center on her mouth. A pulse hammered in her temples as his lazy half-closed look slid back to hold her gaze. There was a disturbing discovery that never in her whole existence had she been so sensually aware of a man as she was at this moment, with the smoothness of the sheets beneath her and the heat of his body burning through the material of her thin pajamas and robe.

The tousled jet black hair invited her to run her fingers through its thickness. The tanned bareness of his chest and shoulders was beneath her hand to explore. Morgan had kissed her before, but always she had struggled either physically or mentally. Now Patty found herself wondering what it would be like to give herself up to the burning mastery of caresses, to glory in the fiery responses she had involuntarily felt before.

In the past, only with Lije had Patty tried to

imagine what it would be like if he made love to her. Hot color swept her cheeks as she realized that it was Morgan who filled her imagination now. Not only filled it, but dominated it with his virility.

Shifting beneath his pressing weight, she pushed the flat of her palm against his shoulder in an effort to free herself from his enervating nearness.

There was a sharp intake of breath and a quick "Careful!" as Morgan winced. Until that second, Patty had forgotten all about his shoulder.

"I'm sorry," she offered swiftly and breathlessly.

The fleeting glimpse of pain was gone. The fire in his gaze ran over her face. His voice took on a low, seductive quality.

"Do you think you can manage a gentle resistance?"

"Morgan —"

Whatever else Patty had intended to say was lost as his mouth tantalized the corners of her sensitive, trembling lips, playing with them until they ached for the light teasing to stop. Instinctively her hand slid up his chest to curl around the back of his neck, the fingers edging into his black, waving hair. When her hand tightened around his neck, his tormenting kisses hardened into possession.

Sanity was abandoned in the chaotic whirl of her emotions. Parting her lips, Morgan explored her mouth, sending fresh waves of desire exploding in her veins. The intimate caress of his hands was awakening her to a stage of sensuality she hadn't dreamed of reaching. She could only gasp at the wonder of it when he pushed the collar of her robe away to bury his head in the hollow of her throat.

"Your heart is racing," Morgan muttered huskily as he dropped kisses around her ear, nibbling at the lobe.

"So — so is yours," Patty whispered, surprised and frightened at the way her arms were clinging to his strong, naked back. Self-consciously she lowered them to a less urgent position near his waist, only to make another discovery. "You — you don't have any clothes on." Her cheeks flamed as she realized how thin the sheet was that separated them.

"You have very few on yourself," he reminded her with a throaty chuckle. "I've compromised you, you know that? My parents would insist that I do the honorable thing and marry you."

"But you don't love me," she protested as he continued to let his mouth roam free around her cheek and ear.

"You don't love me." An invisible shrug

161

accompanied his reply.

Yes, I do, Patty answered silently, qualifying it quickly in her mind that she thought she loved him. At this moment, she seemed dependent on his touch in order to keep her heart beating.

"Your parents don't know I'm here," was the response she gave out loud.

"And if they found us making love, what would you do?" He was nuzzling her neck again.

"I'd . . . I'd be too ashamed to face them."

She felt the tensing of his muscles as he held himself motionless for an instant. Then he raised his head to study her face in the dim light.

"Is that your reaction to my kisses? Shame?" A latent harshness crept into his low voice.

Her heart stopped for an instant and Patty had to close her eyes to keep herself from drawing him back into the closeness of her arms.

"What self-respecting girl would want to be found letting a man who doesn't like her make love to her?" she argued quietly.

Morgan rolled away, lying back on the mattress beside her. "I suppose there is some twisted logic to that observation," he agreed dryly.

Her limbs were still too weak to enable her to move. She turned her head sideways on the pillow to look at him.

"Morgan, why did you kiss me?"

His face was in the shadow so she could only see a dim outline of his rough features.

"I wanted to," he answered calmly. "And I sensed that you wanted me to. You did, didn't you?"

It wasn't exactly a question, but Patty answered it anyway. "Yes, I did."

She levered herself upright before she revealed the nebulous sensation that she had fallen in love with him. She had disliked him for so long that it seemed absurd that she could reverse her emotions in the space of a few minutes.

"Tell me," Morgan commanded. "Did you enjoy it?"

"I wasn't taking notes." Patty tried to shrug away his question.

"I certainly hope not," he chuckled, a pleasant sound that moved caressingly over her skin.

"I have to see grandpa." She slipped from the bed before Morgan could try to stop her.

Her haste was unnecessary as he remained in his prone position. Quickly she secured the robe around her neck, the heat rising in her face under the intensity of his gaze.

"What could be so urgent at this hour?" he questioned with a trace of amusement at her hurried and fumbling movements.

"Landmark was fussing. I thought grandpa should check. I was going to go myself —" If she had, none of this would have happened, Patty realized. All this turmoil wouldn't be disrupting and confusing her now. "I should have," she finished grimly.

"And you're sorry you didn't, aren't you?" Morgan added quietly. "Don't answer that." He inhaled deeply as if to control a growing impatience. "There's no need to waken your grandfather. I'll check on the horses for you."

Patty was about to make some silly protest that she didn't want to bother him, then she changed her mind. The dim light played over his naked chest as he sat up in the bed. Quickly she turned away.

"Would you like me to go with you?" she asked nervously.

There was the rustling of material and the sound of bare legs stepping into Levi's. "I don't think that's a particularly good idea, Patty."

He didn't explain, but then he didn't have to. Patty was aware of the kindled fire inside of her that required only the spark of his touch to be ignited into flame again. For all Morgan's control, he was a man, and that was a dangerous fire to play with.

"Thank you," she murmured.

"For what?" he mocked; cat-quiet footsteps had brought him to her side.

"F-for checking on the horses," Patty stumbled.

A brilliant light still burned in his eyes as he looked down on her with a knowing smile. "I need the fresh air anyway."

Patty knew her attempts to be silent as she felt her way back down the stairs amused Morgan, but at this point she couldn't handle the embarrassment of being discovered.

"Off to bed with you," he murmured near her hair when they reached the ground-floor hallway. "And don't stick your nose outside the door again tonight."

"The horses —" she began.

"If there's any trouble, I'm capable of taking care of it. Now, good-night," Morgan issued firmly.

"Good-night." Patty moved reluctantly toward her room.

CHAPTER EIGHT

Patty hadn't gone immediately to bed when she reached her room. For long moments she had stood at the window gazing at the stables and light that flickered with the movement of the night breeze through the leaves of the tree outside. The absurd sensation that she had fallen in love with the tall, dark-haired man out there in the stables had persisted, but she couldn't reconcile the emotion with all the years of intense dislike.

You couldn't simply dislike a man for that length of time and then one night declare that you loved him, she had argued with herself. It wasn't logical.

With the dawning of the new day, Patty still refused to accept the possibility that she had truly fallen in love with Morgan Kincaid. It was physical desire, she told herself firmly. Her body had simply reacted to his expert caresses. There was no need to try to condone her responses with some ridiculous notion that she loved the man. Morgan Kincaid had attracted her with his virility, that was all. That *had* to be all it was.

The tumbling of her stomach at the sight of him sitting at the breakfast table, dark and vitally attractive, cast the first stone of doubt. She avoided the glittering blue of his eyes as she took her chair.

"Good morning. Did you sleep well?" Molly Kincaid greeted Patty, as she set a glass of orange juice in front of her.

"Yes, thank you, I did." The sudden clamoring of her senses at Morgan's presence made her voice unnaturally tight.

"When she finally got to sleep," Morgan added. There was a faint inflection that made his comment a direct taunt. The half-angry look she gave him was an unspoken plea for his silence that he ignored. "Patty came to my room last night," he explained, his eyes dancing with laughter at the sudden flames in her cheeks. "She heard one of the horses fussing and mistook my room for her grandfather's."

"I thought I heard voices around midnight coming from your room," Everett King declared. "I couldn't make up my mind if I was hearing things or if you were talking in your sleep."

"Was there any problem with the horses?"

Lucas Kincaid glanced at his son.

"No, I checked," Morgan shook his head. "A case of lonesomeness, I guess."

"I'm sorry I woke you unnecessarily," Patty offered stiffly.

"You suitably compensated me at the time," he murmured suggestively, the edges of his mouth twitching in mockery.

Lucas Kincaid gave Patty a look of amused contemplation before exchanging a knowing look with his wife. Patty stared at Morgan in helpless frustration. *Why couldn't he have kept silent about last night,* she cried hopelessly. *Why had he made her accidental visit to his bedroom last night common knowledge?*

"Morgan, stop embarrassing Patty." Molly Kincaid came to her rescue with a mild reprimand.

"Am I?" He studied her downcast gaze and the high color in her face that Patty couldn't control. "You have to admit, mom, that she looks guilty. Anyone would think by looking at her that she'd crawled into bed with me."

Her fingers closed around the orange juice glass, and the urge to throw it into his mocking face trembled violently within her. The gleam in his eyes told her that Morgan had read her mind. The watchful expression in his face was plainly daring her to do it and let everyone see how close his remark had come to the truth.

With quivering control, she picked up the glass and drained the juice. It had no taste. In fact, it barely made it past the choked knot of anger in her throat. Patty felt pain, too, pain that he could make fun of what had happened last night. He probably thought it was amusing the way she had responded without any protest.

"I'm not very hungry, Molly." She addressed his mother with forced evenness. The two women had used their Christian names almost from the first day of her arrival. "I think I'll check on Liberty."

"I've finished," her grandfather announced as she rose from her chair. "I'll walk with you, Patty."

Pausing near the table, she waited for her grandfather. She could hardly run from the room. Unwillingly her gaze swept over Morgan. He was leaning back in his chair, regarding her indolently through half-closed eyes. There was something piercingly thoughtful about the way he looked at her. She guessed he was trying to make up his mind about something, but her expression was not giving him the answer to do so with any amount of certainty.

Then the hand of her grandfather was touching her elbow, his slight frame at her side.

Patty broke free of Morgan's compelling gaze. The increased beat of her heart added to the fear that she had actually fallen in love with him.

Skinny, kid, Annie Oakley — the names he had called her came back to haunt her as she walked from the house to the stables. They were hardly names to indicate that he had formed any romantic attachment to her. No, his lovemaking had only been another way to mock her.

"It was a mistake to come here, gramps," Patty said at last, her steps slowing dispiritedly.

"Morgan?" he questioned softly.

Darting a startled look at his lean face, she thought for a minute that he had guessed, with his usual astuteness, that she was hovering on the brink of falling in love with Morgan, if she hadn't already crossed it. But he hadn't guessed, she could tell.

"His shoulder can't heal soon enough," she remarked, breathing easier that her secret was still safe.

It was true. Patty did want Morgan to leave, and the sooner the better. If she wasn't in love with him, only attracted to him, then she wanted him to leave before it could grow into something more permanent. If it was love that she felt, and she was beginning to suspect the worst, then it was vital that his departure occur soon while the emotion was in its growing stage.

An inner voice told her that the pain she had felt at the demise of her infatuation with Lije was nothing compared to the agony she could go through. Patty was determined to remain free of pain for the rest of her life — or at least not be so foolish again as to fall in love with a man who didn't care for her.

"I'm not going to be able to remain in the same house with him much longer," she murmured in a vague warning.

"He's only teasing," her grandfather smiled without amusement in a conciliatory attempt to ease the frustration that he sensed was seething beneath her controlled calm.

"Then let's just say that I don't appreciate his brand of humor." She frowned quickly at the painful truth of her words.

"I can't very well ask him when he intends to leave," Everett argued logically. "This is his home and we are the ones who are guests."

"Then keep him out of my way!" Patty bit out desperately.

There was a moment of awkward silence as they resumed their course to the stables. Preoccupied, Patty didn't notice it at first. Then she glanced at the solemn face.

"Grandpa, what have you maneuvered me into this time?" she asked warily.

He glanced at her out of the corner of his eye. "Well, you have to understand, girl, I thought you and Morgan were getting along pretty good. The last few days you've seemed to take his joking in your stride."

"What did you do?"

His tanned and wrinkled hand adjusted the stetson hat on his peppery gray head. "Morgan offered to take us into Oklahoma City the day after tomorrow. I'd mentioned how often you and I had talked about going to the Cowboy Hall of Fame. I meant to say something about it to you last night, but I forgot."

"I am not going!" she declared forcefully.

"Patty —"

"I am not going!" she repeated.

"Don't be stubborn now. Listen to me," her grandfather requested in his most persuasive voice.

"Every time I listen to you I find myself getting talked into something. No." Patty shook her head vigorously.

"Have I ever convinced you to do anything that wasn't for the best in the end?"

"In the end," she admitted tightly, tossing him an angry look. "But not at the beginning or the middle."

"It's the way a thing ends up that counts."

Sighing heavily, Patty gave in. "All right. I'll listen, but that doesn't mean I'm going to agree."

There was a decided twinkle of triumph in his brown eyes and Patty knew she shouldn't have allowed her grandfather the smallest foothold. He was like Morgan in that respect. The minute she gave an inch, he took a mile. *But that's what happens when you love someone,* she thought to herself. Her lips tightened at that admission.

"You see," her grandfather began, "Morgan isn't making the trip into Oklahoma City specially for us. He's going there on business. While he's taking care of that, he suggested that we could go to the Hall of Fame. It's not as if you have to spend the entire morning in his company, just the ride there and back. That's no more time than what you would spend at the dinner table. And I'll be there to act as a buffer."

"I'm not going."

In her mind, she was visualizing the journey, sitting in silence in the back seat of the car, mesmerized by the broad shoulders and the black hair that curled around his muscular neck. And the blue eyes that would catch her studying him in the mirror and glitter with knowing mockery.

"You're being stubborn," her grandfather murmured.

"So are you. After all, it's not imperative that we see the Hall of Fame now," Patty argued. "You and I can drive to Oklahoma City anytime by ourselves. It's not that far. When Morgan leaves, we can make a day of it."

She considered her arguments to be based on sound logic, but she had forgotten her grandfather was just as stubborn as she was, especially if he believed he was right. For the next thirty-six hours he kept up a subtle barrage of comments, chiseling patiently away at her adamant stand until Patty toppled and agreed.

On Thursday morning, she was at the breakfast table, dressed in a summery cotton dress of sunny yellow, trying to convince herself that she had worn it because she was going into the city and not because she wanted to impress Morgan with her feminine curves that the dress showed off so well.

Patty even took pains to avoid his glance, in case he commented on her appearance, a decided change from her usual Levi's and top. But Morgan was unusually silent, barely speaking at all during the morning meal.

Not until they were walking from the house to the ranch's station wagon did he address a

174

remark directly to her. "I didn't think you were going to come," he said with casual interest.

Patty glanced at her grandfather, several steps in front of them, a poisonous dart in the look as she guessed he had mentioned her initial refusal.

"Neither did I," she retorted.

"Your grandfather made me promise to be on my best behavior."

Flushing self-consciously, she kept her gaze downcast. She didn't want to make any reply, but she knew she had to, for pride's sake.

"And are you?"

"Going to be on my best behavior?" he finished the question, turning his dark head to look at her. Shrugging, he answered, "It's going to be difficult."

"It's not so difficult," Patty said, keeping her gaze fixed on the car, refusing to let it waver to the compelling man at her side. "We can simply ignore each other."

"It's not easy to ignore you."

His softly spoken reply drew her gaze like a magnet. Something in his voice insisted that she look at him. A slow, lazy smile was spreading across his face, crinkling the corners of his eyes. Patty caught at her breath, very nearly running back to the house before the pull of his charm became irresistible. She wished her grandfather had never extracted that promise from him. She would rather have endured Morgan's mocking insults than be exposed to this potent and compromising friendliness.

"I don't find it difficult to ignore you," she declared cuttingly, sharply averting her gaze.

"I've noticed that — at times," Morgan agreed dryly, placing significant emphasis on the qualifying "at times."

Yes, there had been times when his touch and kiss had obliterated all thought of anyone or anything else. The silent acknowledgment was accompanied by a betraying warmth rising in her neck. Patty quickened her steps to give herself time to control the revealing blush free of his inspecting eye.

Her grandfather was holding the door to the back seat of the station wagon open for her and Patty slipped quickly in. She made a pretense of adjusting the flared skirt of her dress as the driver's door opened.

"There's plenty of room in the front, Patty." Silent laughter ran through Morgan's voice. "You don't have to sit back there by yourself."

In the front seat, Patty knew she would be placed in the middle between the two men, in constant physical contact with Morgan for the whole of the ride to Oklahoma City.

"I'm perfectly comfortable here, thank you,"

she insisted, putting a chill in her voice that Morgan couldn't overlook.

"Suit yourself," he shrugged, and slid behind the wheel.

Her heart sank as the car was started and driven away from the house around the circular drive and down the lane to the highway. She was miserable. The last thing she wanted to do was to be snappish and standoffish, but it was the only way she knew to keep Morgan at a distance. Not that he wanted to be any closer; she was the one who wanted that.

Forcing her attention away from the dark, curling black head in front of her, she tried to concentrate on the undulating hills with their green dots of trees. In some ways, the landscape of the ranch was reminiscent of her own home in New Mexico. Patty would have liked to explore it on horseback, but it was better that she wasn't too familiar with Morgan's home. Better for her peace of mind, at least.

How long would it be before Morgan returned to the rodeo circuit, she wondered. Initially his statement had been that he was going to take a two-week rest. That was more than half gone. He had removed the sling three days ago, although his shoulder still wasn't capable of heavy work.

When he was gone, then what? She and her

grandfather were supposed to stay another two months more or less. Thus far, Patty had been subjected to a minimum of stories from Morgan's parents about his childhood days. He was their son. It was natural for them to talk about him. What a mistake it had been to come here, Patty thought dejectedly.

Nervously nibbling at her lower lip, she caught the movement of Morgan's head as he half turned it toward her, revealing his strong, jutting profile, powerfully carved and rugged. His blue gaze left the road in front of them long enough to flick briefly at her.

"What do you know about Oklahoma?" he asked.

"The usual," Patty shrugged, watching the traffic zooming along the expressway.

"There are quite a few interesting places to visit within easy distance of the ranch. You and Everett should do some exploring while you're here."

"We might do that," she agreed tautly.

"To the east of Ardmore is a small town called Tishomingo. It's the site of a major wildlife refuge and the headquarters of one of the Five Civilized Nations," suggested Morgan.

"Indian tribes?" she queried, biting her lip the instant the question was out, wishing she had let the conversation die its own death.

"Yes, Indian tribes," he replied with patient humor. "The Cherokee, Chickasaw, Choctaw, Creek and Seminole Indians are known as the Five Civilized Nations. I'm sure you're aware that Oklahoma was originally the Indian Territory. Originally, sixty-seven tribes were transported to reservations here. But a lot of the credit for the development of the Indian Territory into the State of Oklahoma belongs to the Five Civilized Nations. When they arrived, they brought with them an advanced system of education and a complex tribal organization and government as well as Christianity. It was their leadership that truly organized the Indian Territory."

"I didn't know that," Patty murmured, her tone self-conscious.

"The first newspaper in Oklahoma was the *Cherokee Advocate,* published in Tahlequah, Oklahoma, the capital of the Cherokee Nation."

The expressway on which they were traveling began to climb into the Arbuckle Mountains, monoliths that were weathered and rounded by time, sand-colored rocks thrust out here and there or exposed in sheer cliffs where the concrete road carved its way through.

Morgan pointed out the exit to Turner Falls, explaining that there were two large swimming areas near the base of the famous waterfall as

179

well as a campground and picnic facilities. On the north side of the Arbuckles were the rolling flatlands.

"Pauls Valley," Morgan identified the town they were approaching. "The last Saturday in June the World Championship Watermelon Seed Spitting contest is held here."

In spite of herself, Patty smiled, carving dimples in her cheeks. Morgan caught the brief look she darted at his reflection in the rearview mirror, a suggestion of an encouraging smile around his mouth. He was arousing her interest and he knew it. She had the distinct feeling that he was determined that she enjoy the trip, although she didn't know why he should care.

"I'm not boring you with my trivia, am I?" he asked.

There was a slight negative movement of her head. "No," she responded.

"I know gramps coerced you into this trip." Morgan darted a look at the older man who was trying to be as unobtrusive as possible. "Since you are gallantly tolerating my company, I thought the least I could do was to be as informative as I could."

He had read her thoughts again and was gently, and mockingly, letting her know that he had. As long as he didn't read any more than that, Patty didn't mind.

"I thought there was a purpose behind your history lesson," she replied.

"If you want to go back in history," he said, checking for traffic before edging into the passing lane to go by a slow-moving truck, "then you should visit the Heavener Runestone State Park in eastern Oklahoma."

"What's that?" her grandfather asked, Morgan's glance ending his self-imposed silence.

"More than four hundred years before Columbus supposedly discovered America, some Norse explorers traveled through that section of the state and marked their passage by carving runes, characters from their runic alphabet, onto a stone."

During the rest of the trip into Oklahoma City, Morgan told them about the cattle trails that had crossed the state, the Chisholm and the Western Trails and the Butterfield Overland Southern Mail. He talked about the government land rushes that opened the Indian lands to homesteaders.

Then they crossed the bridge over the Canadian River, skirted Norman, Oklahoma, and entered the city limits of Oklahoma City. Leaving the expressway, Morgan took a route through the city streets to the state capitol grounds. As the domeless capitol building came into view, he glanced in the mirror at Patty's reflection.

"The only state capitol in the world with an oil well underneath it," he smiled.

His statement was unnecessary. The steel derrick almost directly in front of the columned portico entrance to the gray stone structure spoke for itself. More derricks were dotted throughout the capitol grounds, straddling pumps that monotonously bobbed their heads up and down to extract the precious oil from beneath the surface.

At the north edge of the city, Morgan drew their attention to a hill looking over the downtown section. He turned onto the street that lay at its base. The white peaks of a roofed structure were visible on the top of the hill, along with flags snapping in the wind.

"That is Persimmon Hill and the National Cowboy Hall of Fame on top of it. One of the branches of the Chisholm Trail used to run along the foot of the hill," Morgan explained. From the street at the base, he turned onto a side street and onto another that climbed the mountain. "The flag esplanade on the side displays the flags of the seventeen Western states that built and sponsored this national memorial to the cowboy, as well as the United States flag."

Bypassing the parking area, he drove close to

the walk leading to the entrance and stopped. Patty was halfway out of the car when the hand she placed on the opened door for balance was taken by Morgan. She found herself trapped in a triangle, the car, the door and a set of broad shoulders forming the three sides.

For a paralyzing instant, she stood immobile, her head tilted back, her brown eyes staring into his impassive face. Mockery glinted in the blue depths of his eyes, sootily outlined with dark lashes. Morgan made no move to let her pass, while her heart hammered like the trapped bird she was.

"Well?" A brow arched complacently.

"Well what?" Patty frowned.

"Did I keep my promise or not?"

"What promise?" She was too disturbed by his nearness to think straight.

"That I'd be on my best behavior." He ran a dancing eye over her.

Her tongue moved nervously over her suddenly parched lips. She regretted the stalling gesture immediately as Morgan's attention shifted to her lips. Her senses quivered in response, but the deliciously pleasant reaction was not one that she wanted to feel.

"Yes, I suppose you were," she murmured, wondering if he noticed the slight breathiness in her voice.

"You don't sound certain."

"The trip isn't over yet." Her response was meant to come out cold and sharp, instead it was weak and apprehensive.

"What are you afraid of, Skinny?" he asked thoughtfully.

She gained a hold on her composure and gripped it tightly. "That's absurd. I'm not afraid of anything. Now let me pass."

"Something is troubling you. It's there in your eyes." His gaze narrowed, trying to pierce through her fragile mask of pride. "What is it? An attack of melancholy? Or homesickness?"

"Maybe I'm simply tired of fencing words with you." Despite the pressure of his fingers, she yanked her hand free of his. "I'm entitled to the privacy of my thoughts and I certainly don't intend to confide them to you."

"I do make you angry, don't I?" Morgan smiled.

"Yes, you do!" Patty glared. "I think you enjoy making me lose my temper."

"It's better than seeing you wasting your time mooning over Lije Masters," he shrugged complacently, and stepped to one side.

"I don't want to hear you say his name again!" she flashed.

"When are you going to get over that ridiculous infatuation?"

184

I am over it, Patty wanted to shout. But of course she couldn't. He might ask how and why. And the answers to those two questions were all tied up with her feelings for him.

"I've told you before," she said instead, "that I wish Lije all the happiness in the world. What more do you want?"

"It's not what I want that counts. It's what you want," countered Morgan.

"At the moment all I want is to tour the Cowboy Hall of Fame," Patty snapped.

"Nothing's stopping you." He glanced at the open passageway between himself and the car, and Patty walked hurriedly past him. "My business is going to take me a couple of hours, so the two of you can take your time."

"We intend to," Patty shot back, darting an angry glance at her grandfather for leaving her to Morgan's mercy and not attempting to rescue her.

Chapter Nine

Despite her boastful brags to the contrary, Patty raced through the first part of the exhibits and had to retrace her steps to see it again. It seemed impossible that her emotions could be in such a turmoil, so contradictory. While she had been quivering with desire to know Morgan's love, she had been shouting at him in anger. Or had it been frustration?

Her confusion was eased or at least distracted as she studied the art and sculpture exhibit with its renowned works of the great Western Art masters, including Russell and Remington. The National Rodeo Hall of Fame section she toured with her grandfather, enjoying his accounts of some of the rodeo contestants he had known, always conscious of the life-size replica of Russell's "Bronc-Twister" that dominated that section.

Finally Patty went to the last exhibit, the pure, gleaming white statue called "End of the Trail," symbolizing the end of the frontier and the life-style of the Indian. No matter from what angle she viewed the massive work, sitting on its matching white pedestal, it dominated and awed her. Strangely it stood out against its background of glass walls and steeply sloping white ceilings.

"It's impressive, isn't it?"

Patty had not paid any attention to the footsteps behind her, thinking it was another visitor like herself. A startled look over her shoulder was returned by Morgan's bland gaze before he reverted it to the statue. His hands were slipped casually in his pockets, his stand relaxed. Patty felt as taut as a high tension wire.

"Is it that late already?" She glanced at her watch. More than two hours had passed, closer to three.

"I haven't been here but a few minutes," he assured her calmly. "My business took longer than I anticipated. I was afraid you were waiting for me."

"Grandpa —"

"I've already seen him," Morgan interrupted. "He told me where you were."

"If you'd like to leave now —" Patty began. She couldn't summon any coldness. He had caught her by surprise and her responses were stilted and nervous.

"No hurry." He brought his gaze from the

187

statue to her face. "Have you seen the fountains?"

"Only from the windows."

"Let's go outside, then."

His fingers lightly closed around her elbow and guided her toward a glass exit door. Strolling around the walk, they followed the bridge walk that meandered over the fountain pools. The water shimmered a pale blue, reflecting the color of the milky sky. Here and there jets of water sprayed into the air. Once by the pools, Morgan directed her along a path to the point of the wooded hill. There they stopped and gazed back at the modern structure.

"The building was designed to symbolize the tents used by the early settlers. At night, with the light radiating from the center, it resembles a tent encampment around a camp fire," Morgan explained. "The fountains and pools are reminders of how very vital water was to the pioneers. The glass walls are to remind you of the vast spaciousness of the West."

"It's beautiful," Patty murmured.

Morgan nodded and guided her toward the graves on the overlooking nob of Persimmon Hill where some of the famous bucking horses were buried – Midnight, Five Minutes to Midnight, and others. There Patty paused, resting a hand against a tree and looking out over the valley below.

"It's quite a view."

"Nothing like what the eighty-niners saw," he agreed.

His voice came from directly behind her, but Patty's sensitive radar had already signaled his nearness. She moved closer to the tree, leaning slightly against it for support.

"Shouldn't we be leaving?" she asked.

"Everett is going to join us out here when he's finished." Morgan braced an arm against the tree trunk, his hand inches from her head, but his gaze was on the city below.

A dangerous lethargy was seeping into her limbs. Patty shifted away from the trunk and Morgan.

"I'd better see what's keeping grandpa."

"I said he'd be along." His blue gaze swerved to lock onto hers.

"I know, but —"

"But you can't stand to be in my company another minute, isn't that right?" Morgan asked smoothly.

His lack of anger or mockery was unexpected. The expression in his face only revealed a calm acceptance of his statement.

"Not really," Patty contradicted him, even though it was true.

"I have some news that should bring a smile

to your face," he continued without acknowledging her reply. "I'll be joining up with my brother on Sunday. He's going to help me with the rodeo stock for a week, then come back."

"But I thought —" Frowning with surprise, she began to remind him that the two weeks weren't up yet.

Again Morgan ignored her words. "That calls for a celebration, doesn't it?" he smiled, a casual easy smile without any bitterness or taunting anger.

"That's unfair," Patty breathed, turning from him to stare sightlessly at the city below.

"Face it, Skinny, we're just making each other's lives miserable," he said quietly. "We're always at each other's throats in one way or another. You're not going to change and I won't."

Her hands were clenched into fists at her side, her fingers digging into the palms to keep the tears from filling her eyes.

"If you wouldn't make fun of me all the time," she began.

"And if you weren't so stubborn and proud," he supplied with a trace of humor. "There isn't anything we can agree on. All our conversations end in an argument of some sort."

"That's because you —"

"See what I mean?" Morgan queried lightly.

190

"Already you're starting to argue. You told me once that you were tired of this constant state of war between us. Well, we can never be friends." His dark head moved to the side in negative resignment. "I couldn't make that transition after all this time."

His compelling look was asking her a question. "Neither could I." Patty accepted at last that she loved him, fully and completely. To be just his friend would be bitterly intolerable.

"But I admit that I'm tired of the fighting, too." His gaze swept the skies, then concentrated on some distant cloud. "But I also admit that I can't ignore you. Whenever you're around, the sparks are there, the friction. So I'm leaving, ahead of schedule."

"You've made this decision rather suddenly, haven't you?" She stared at the same cloud, a coldness in her heart.

"It's been building for some time, but I kept thinking something would change, if only for your grandfather's sake. I tried today to be impersonal and friendly, but it didn't work. So I'm getting out of the picture."

"I'm sorry, Morgan."

"Be sorry for yourself." He refused her faint apology. "You're the one who wants to live with ghosts for the rest of your life and you're too stubborn to open your eyes to see what else the world might have to offer."

"I do not —" Pain flickered in her brown eyes as she instinctively raised her voice.

"I take it back." His hand raised to hold off the rest of her denial. "I take back what I said. Our last private conversation is not going to end in an argument."

White teeth bit into her trembling lower lip before Patty exhaled a shaky sigh. "Yes," she agreed. "We should be capable of that."

"Here comes Everett." Morgan pushed his hands into his pockets and turned toward the lean older man walking their way.

A strange brooding silence hung over the Kincaid ranch on their return, one that had begun on their journey and remained to throw a dark cloud over Morgan's last two days. It was an atmosphere that everyone noticed and no one commented on.

For those same two days, Patty had carefully rehearsed the goodbye speech she was going to give to Morgan, a hopeful attempt to keep the door between them from closing permanently. When she came down to breakfast Sunday morning, she discovered that Morgan had left two hours earlier.

"But he didn't even say goodbye," she murmured in an unconscious protest.

"He told us," Molly Kincaid replied, "that

the two of you had already said all there was to say." She hesitated, then added quietly, "I'm sorry, Patty."

Patty's fingers clasped the edge of the table as she stared at the coffee cup in front of her. "It doesn't matter," she replied tightly.

But it did matter. It mattered very much. The backs of her eyes were being scorched with tears. Any second now they would tumble into view. She pushed herself away from the table, mumbling a polite permission to be excused as she rose to her feet and hurried to the door.

In the solitude of the stables, the burning tears refused to flow while acid pain ate away at her heart. Her hand unconsciously caressed the butting head of a white horse, not even aware of which horse it was stroking.

"I think Lodestar could do with some exercise." Her grandfather's voice spoke quietly at her side.

She stared into the luminous brown eyes of the white horse. "You know why he left, don't you, Grandpa? It was because of me."

There was no need to identify Morgan. Everett King knew whom she was talking about.

"I guessed that," acknowledged Everett King. "His parents?"

"I think they knew the reason, too."

The muscles in her throat constricted into a

near stranglehold. She forced herself to swallow, lessening her throat's grip but not the knot in her stomach.

"I feel awful." She closed her eyes and rested he head against the horse's forelock. "How do you put up with me, gramps?"

"I love you," he replied simply.

"I'm sorry," she murmured.

"Why? Grandfathers are supposed to love their granddaughters," he teased, a sympathetic twinkle lighting his brown eyes.

"You must be so ashamed of me," Patty sighed.

"You can't help the way you feel toward Morgan any more than he can," he said quietly. "I must admit that I had hoped you might bury your dislike."

She started to explain that she loved Morgan, then stopped. Her grandfather had shared so much of her pain when Lije married. It wasn't fair to ask him to shoulder more of her misery. She was an adult, a woman. It was time she stopped carrying her tears to others and faced the consequences of her actions alone.

"I — I think I'll take Lodestar out," she faltered.

"That's a good idea."

The days trickled by with the slowness of grains of sand in an hourglass. Patty worked with the horses to the point of exhaustion, collapsing in bed at nights to cry herself to sleep. Her appetite was nonexistent and she lost weight. Her laughter, when it was reluctantly summoned, was hollow and without its usual zest.

To her grandfather's concerned queries, she merely shrugged that she was fine. But the frown of worry was almost perpetually lining his forehead.

One day he had asked pointedly, "Is it still Lije? Are you still breaking your heart over him?"

The rhythmic stroke of the currycomb hadn't paused as Patty had made her reply deliberately ambiguous. "You don't stop caring for someone simply because they don't care for you."

Her grandfather had sighed and walked away, his peppered gray head shaking sadly. From that day on, she had truly tried to regain her former buoyant spirits to ease her grandfather's mind. But she didn't think she had fooled him. Two months later, she was driving the pickup that pulled their travel trailer through the entrance gate of the rodeo grounds. Until the moment she saw the stock truck and the bold letters Kincaid Rodeo Company, Patty hadn't realized how much she had been anticipating the moment when she would see Morgan again. Out of sight had never made him out of mind.

Her eyes searched the Western-clad figures for a glimpse of his ebony black hair and broad shoulders. But he was nowhere to be seen. There were plenty of welcoming shouts and waves as their van and trailer were recognized, but no sign of Morgan. He had known they would be coming. Her grandfather had telephoned last week to confirm that they would be keeping the engagement.

As the disappointment and depression set in, Patty realized that secretly she had been praying that Morgan would be there to welcome them back — if not her, then at least her grandfather. Hope was a difficult emotion to ignore.

All the while they were unloading the horses and settling them into the stall, she kept watching for him, trying to convince herself that the minute the word reached him that they had arrived he would come to greet them. News traveled fast around the rodeo grounds. Too many people stopped by especially to welcome her and her grandfather back to the circuit. Finally she would pretend no longer that Morgan didn't know they were there. He knew, but he just didn't care.

The bitter taste of rejection nearly gagged her

as she walked to the trailer. She felt physically sick and utterly beaten. The pain in her heart that she had been certain couldn't get any worse throbbed with excruciating agony. She wanted to do nothing more than throw herself onto her bed and die, but she forced herself to go through the motions of putting the trailer in order.

Sitting at the small table, her cheeks cupped in her hands, Patty saw her grandfather's lean figure making its way toward the trailer. She breathed in deeply, ordering the self-pity to leave. For his sake she must keep up appearances, smile and be happy.

The pot was on the stove, fresh coffee warming on the low flame. She rose from the small couch to pour him a cup. Through the window, she saw him stop in midstride and turn around. Wild joy leaped into her heart as Morgan came into view, a broad smile of welcome flashing across his ruggedly powerful face. The warm handshake, the friendly clasping of shoulders were seen but not noticed. She was drinking in the sight of him, her heart filling with the fullness of her love.

Then the smile vanished from his face, his expression hardening as he glanced at the trailer. His head moved to the side in curt refusal. An invisible knife was plunged into

Patty's stomach. It didn't take much intelligence to guess that her grandfather had invited him to the trailer, no doubt informing him at the same time that she was there. Morgan had no desire to see her.

For an instant, Patty submitted to the surge of pride that rooted her to the floor, the pride that insisted that if he didn't want to speak to her, she didn't want to speak to him. But it had always been her pride that had stood in her way, blinding her for so long from the truth that she loved him, always adding fuel to the animosity between them.

Ignoring the jelly sensation in her legs, Patty walked to the door and opened it, fixing a smile of greeting on her face as she stepped outside. The metallic glint in the gaze that met hers nearly sent her back inside, but she gathered her courage and walked forward.

"Hello, Morgan." Her voice was deliberately controlled to conceal the inner gladness that had no hope of being returned.

"Hello, Patty," he replied in a clipped tone.

For the first time in her life, she would have welcomed Skinny, or kid, or any of the other nicknames he had used. The impersonal use of her name was like a bucket of cold water. He looked at her as if she were a nodding acquaintance.

"Excuse me a minute." Everett King touched her arm, seemingly oblivious to the coolness in the air. "I want to go and say hello to Lefty."

Her eyes left Morgan's face long enough to see the grizzled man hobbling alongside one of the pens. Then her grandfather was walking away, lifting a hand in greeting and calling to his friend. Her gaze slid apprehensively back to Morgan.

"You're looking well, Morgan." Trite words, but the only ones her stilted tongue could speak.

The line of his mouth thinned. "Thank you." Again the clipped response.

Her nerve was slowly beginning to shatter. "Your mother sent her love and — this." Patty had barely touched her fingers on his chest, starting to rise on tiptoe to plant a kiss on his cheek when his fingers were digging into the bones of her shoulders, roughly pushing her away.

"You don't need to transmit the message literally," he snapped.

What had she hoped? That at the touch of her lips Morgan would fold her into his arms and sweep away the barriers with the mastery of his kiss? Why had she so foolishly exposed herself to his rejection? She buried her chin in her neck.

"I thought . . . hoped things had changed," she murmured.

"We aren't friends, Patty." Sardonic laughter punctuated his words. "Let's not pretend that we are."

"I wasn't," she defended softly.

"Of course, you were only delivering a message from my mother. I'd forgotten how very faithful you can be to your misguided sense of duty," he mocked harshly. "Your single-minded devotion must be a by-product of your stubbornness. You're like a bulldog. Once you get hold of an idea, you won't let go even when you know it's wrong."

"You don't know everything, Morgan Kincaid," Patty flashed tiredly.

"At least I don't keep feeding a hope that I know will never bear fruit," Morgan jeered.

"I don't need you to preach to me!"

"Well, you need somebody!" Then he clamped his mouth tightly shut and directed the blazing fires of his gaze to the side. "Nothing has changed," he said in a quieter and grimmer voice. "Five minutes and we're yelling."

Her retaliatory temper vanished. "Morgan —" An apology formed.

"Tell your grandfather I'll talk to him later," he cut in with a heavy sigh, and turned away.

Dejectedly Patty returned to the trailer. The wish that they might find some ground of neutrality was gone. Before their arguments had only served to anger her further. Now the harshness of their exchange hurt deeply. And, as Morgan had said, the sparks seemed inevitable. If she wanted to avoid further heated words, she would have to avoid him. But her love drew her to him unconsciously. And how could she avoid someone that she was likely to run into around any corner of the rodeo grounds?

The next morning's practice rehearsal was flawless. The horses were at peak form, their injuries healed and back in top condition. The only lasting effect had been the lessening of Liberty's speed, but her grandfather had compensated for that by switching his lead position to Landmark's wheel spot.

"They're ready for tonight, gramps!" Patty declared with a satisfied smile as she halted them at the arena gate and vaulted to the ground.

"They're eager, too," Everett King agreed, patting the snorting nose of Landmark. "It's hard to believe the accident ever happened."

"Hey, Princess!" Jack Evans was climbing the arena gate and hopping to the ground. "I heard you were back." He winked as he put an arm around her shoulders and squeezed her tightly. "I missed you."

"I bet there was some pretty blonde around to console you," Patty laughed.

"She never takes me seriously." The comment was addressed to her grandfather with a mock frown.

"I wonder why," he murmured dryly.

"Are you going with me to the big doings Sunday night?" Jack ignored the remark by her grandfather to smile widely at Patty.

"What big doings?" she stalled, a ghost of a smile dimpling her cheeks.

"For Morgan, of course."

Unconsciously, she stiffened, the faint smile vanishing completely. "Morgan?"

"Sure, Morgan," he nodded firmly. "Haven't you heard the news?"

"I g-guess not." She glanced uncertainly at her grandfather.

"He's sold out — lock, stock and barrel to a rodeo outfit out of Dallas," Jack explained.

"You — you must be mistaken," Patty frowned her disbelief.

"No, it's a fact. The new owner is taking over on Monday. Morgan's not even going to finish out the season. So we're throwing him a farewell party Sunday night."

"Did you know about this, Grandpa?"

He didn't squarely meet her questioning look. "I'd heard talk," Everett King hedged.

Patty shook her head. "I don't believe it."

"Well, there's the man," Jack shrugged. "You can ask him yourself."

Morgan was standing at the far end of the corridor that led to the arena gates, talking to one of the local rodeo promoters. As Patty followed Jack's look, she saw Morgan touch a hand to his hat and turn away from the man.

"I will ask him," she said determinedly.

Scrambling over the gate, she ran down the corridor after the retreating broad back. She called to him once and he stopped and turned, his hands moving to his hips in silent challenge. She halted a few feet in front of him, her eyes searching his inscrutable expression.

"Is it true?" she asked in a voice slightly breathless from her run.

"Is what true?" Morgan countered blandly.

"That you're selling out?"

"Yes." He turned and began walking away. His long strides almost forced her into a trot in order to keep up with him.

"You've sold everything? The horses, the bulls, the stock trucks?"

"Everything except Red River," Morgan replied, referring to the aging bucking horse that was to retire this year. "I'm taking him back to the ranch with me and turning him out to pasture."

"Why?"

"Why what?"

"Why are you selling?" Patty asked.

"I've been thinking about quitting for quite a while. Since Alex doesn't want to travel with his wife and family and Dad is getting too old, we decided to sell," he explained in the same unemotional tone that he had used before.

"But why now? Why not finish out the season?" she persisted.

Morgan stopped and faced her, the hard remoteness of steel in the eyes that held hers. "You once indicated that this circuit wasn't big enough for both of us. I've come to the conclusion that you're right." There was a cynical twist to his mouth. "Isn't it a pity that you didn't wait another week before coming back? Then we wouldn't have had to see each other again."

Patty breathed in sharply at his cutting jeer. One dilemma had been solved — how to avoid meeting Morgan. It was confirmed. He was selling and she was supposed to be rejoicing at the news. That was what he expected. With a belligerently defiant toss of her head, Patty confirmed his opinion.

"I'm glad I'm here now instead," she retorted.

"This way I can dance at your farewell party."

"Bring some champagne. It's going to be a night to celebrate," Morgan agreed, a muscle twitching uncontrollably in his jaw. "We can drink a toast when they play 'Auld Lang Syne.'"

"I'll bring a whole case of champagne!" she vowed. "Just don't expect me to join in the chorus of 'For He's A Jolly Good Fellow.'"

"Whatever you do," he muttered beneath his breath, "please don't make my last days here pleasant ones. I'd hate to ruin a perfect record."

Her hand connected with his cheek in a resounding slap. Before he could retaliate, she was stalking away, tears streaming down her face.

CHAPTER TEN

From a stranger's point of view, Morgan's farewell party was a huge success. A local tavern had been reserved exclusively for the celebration. There was music and laughter, hoorahing and backslapping, plenty of food and drink for an army.

Patty was one of the last to arrive. She had turned down Jack's invitation to the party, choosing to go with her grandfather instead. If she hadn't been certain that Morgan would notice her absence, she wouldn't have gone at all. At least with her grandfather, she could leave when she pleased and not be dependent upon a fun-loving date to take her home.

It wasn't easy to adopt a jubilant attitude, not when her heart was sick at Morgan's leaving. Only knowing how much he wanted to be away from her enabled her to do it with her head held proudly in the air.

She only faltered once — when he had proposed a toast to her.

"To Patty King, alias Annie Oakley, the fastest tongue in the West. May she rest in peace," Morgan had proclaimed with mocking laughter, and downed the contents of his glass.

She hadn't been able to lift her own glass to her lips. She hadn't been able to break away from the savage glitter of his gaze. Within seconds, her grandfather was at her side, gently leading her away from Morgan's table.

"He hates me, grandpa," Patty had whispered as he led her out the door.

"No, gal," he had replied quietly, putting a comforting arm around her shoulder. "It just seems that way."

When the sun blinked into her window the next morning, it was hard to accept that he was really gone, that he had left at daybreak. She and her grandfather were staying over another day before traveling to their next stop on the circuit. He wanted the horses to have one full day of rest before trailering them on a long drive.

At the stables, Patty learned from Lefty that the new owner of the rodeo stock was keeping them over one more day as well — not to rest the animals, but to complete the installation of his managers and chute bosses and to test out some horses that a couple of local ranchers had brought in.

A few minutes after Lefty had gone, Jack Evans leaned over the stall door where Patty was currying Lodestar.

"Some local bronc busters think they have some rough, tough horses, and I've volunteered to top them off for them. Why don't you come on down and watch?"

"I don't feel like it, Jack. Some other time maybe." She wanted to be left alone.

But Jack wasn't the type to take no for an answer. He opened the stall door and walked in, taking the currycomb from her hand at the same time that he grasped her by the wrist.

"Those stupid old horses of yours can wait. You and I are going to the arena and have some fun," he announced.

"But, Jack —" Patty protested as he continued to drag her along with him.

"You turned me down flat to that party last night," he reminded her. "Now you gotta make up for it."

"I think you partied too much last night," she said with thinly disguised exasperation.

"I could be stone-drunk and still ride those mangy-tailed excuses of horses. Even you could ride one of these 'wild' horses." His eyes widened with mock fear as he emphasized the wild. "You come watch me and I'll buy you breakfast."

They were nearly at the arena. "Do I have much choice?" Patty asked, sighing as she accepted her fate.

"None at all, my princess," Jack grinned back at her, drawing a reluctant smile in return.

There were a dozen or so cowboys perched on the rails of the arena near the chutes. Half a dozen more were working behind the chutes running the ranch horses into the partitioned runway, dropping the gates as each one was at its designated place, trapping them inside.

"Hey, Rafe!" Jack called. "Have you got my rigging with you?"

One of the men in back of the chutes waved that he had.

While Patty found herself a seat on the top rail, Jack made his way to the first chute where a horse was haltered and ready for the saddle. Working in the close quarters of a chute, the saddling and flanking of a horse was something that was never hurried. But experience made the procedure swift and sure. A few minutes later, Jack was sitting deep in the saddle, his hat crammed tightly on his head, his blunted spurs lying along the horse's neck, one hand on the rope and the other in the air. A quick nod to the man on the chute gate and it was swung open with an accompanying, "Let 'er buck!"

The horse bucked, but even Patty's less than

experienced eye could see that it was not of the caliber of the rodeo horses. It wasn't a genuine bucker, just a rank horse that needed to be shown who was boss. Before the bell signaled the end of the ride, the horse was only buck jumping around the arena. Jack waved off the pickup riders and jumped from the horse, landing on his feet with a flourish of his hand.

"How was that, Princess?" He ambled cockily to the fence, a wide grin of triumph on his face. "I told you it would be a snap. Do you want to try one?" Before she had a chance to respond, he was turning away.

"Paul, do you care if Patty here tries out one of your horses?"

The man named Paul shook his head that he didn't mind and went back to his conversation with two men who appeared to be the owners of the horses in question.

"Eddy," Jack waved to one of the men on the fence rail, "Patty's going to ride."

Then he was taking her hand and helping her down from the rail, taking it for granted that she intended to ride. In sort of numbed shock, she followed him without protest. Unbidden the thought came that if Morgan had been here, he would have hit the ceiling.

But Morgan wasn't there anymore. He couldn't order her around and curse her for being fifty kinds of a fool.

As Patty climbed up the sides of the chute where a Roman-nosed buckskin was held, she knew she was going to ride, a last symbolic gesture that Morgan's presence did not intimidate her life any longer.

It was crazy. It was stupid. But she was going to do it.

She had the best in the business instructing her. And for all of Jack's wildness and cockiness, he was one of the top saddle bronc riders in rodeo and had been for several years. When he stood above the chutes, he was all professional. Now that he had her at the chutes, he wasn't rushing her.

"Let Sam go out first on that sorrel. We're going to take a few minutes," he ordered crisply, then turned to Patty and smiled. "Are you nervous, Princess?"

"A little," she admitted.

He winked and smiled broadly, his vague excitement contagious, "Take a few deep breaths," he ordered.

While Jack supervised the saddling, two chutes down from them, the gate swung open for the rider named Sam. His horse stood in frozen stillness in the chute. Finally after much pushing, shoving and hat waving, it trotted out, gave a few half-hearted jumps, and hurried to the side gate that would take it back to the pens and the rest of its companions, to the boos of the spectators.

"Okay, Princess." Jack signaled that they were ready for her. Patty stood above the horse, her feet on the inside chute rails. "You're going to ride this horse all the way. Don't you forget that." Patty knew confidence was the keynote and nodded. "When you settle into that saddle, be quiet and firm. Let him know you're boss. Get your feet in the stirrups and get set. We want to swing the gate open and give you some elbowroom as soon as you're ready. Old Buck here is supposed to be a straight-out, honest bucker with no fancy tricks."

Patty nodded again, not quite capable of speech. Balance, timing and nerve were what she needed in the arena. Two out of three wasn't bad, she thought with an inward smile.

Taking a last deep breath, she started to lower herself into the saddle, a feeling of exhilaration beginning to bring her dead senses alive as the adrenalin began to flow. She had blocked out the sounds of the other men around the chutes, listening only to Jack.

Then, from behind her, came a savagely muttered, "What the hell do you think you're doing?"

Her heart leaped into her dry throat at the

familiar voice. She didn't have a chance to turn her head before an iron band was circling her stomach and lifting her out of the chute. As if she were a weightless object, she was swung over the top rail and lowered to the arena ground with Morgan a half step behind her.

He towered above her, hands on his hips, his expression unyielding in its harshness. "You can't even let me leave this place before you're trying to break your fool neck with some other fool stunt!" he shouted.

The anger blazing in Morgan's voice and eyes triggered Patty's own temper. Her booted foot stamped the ground as she returned his glare with defiant fury.

"It's my neck and I can break it if I want to, Morgan Kincaid!"

"I'll be damned if you will!" he snapped.

"You haven't any right to tell me what to do. Now get out of my way!" Tears of anger and humiliation burned her eyes as she tried to push her way past Morgan. She was too aware of their amused audience of cowboys to let him order her about like a child.

But the granite wall wasn't to be pushed aside and she found herself imprisoned by his grip, his fingers digging into the soft flesh of her arms.

"You're not getting on that horse!" he told

213

her harshly, ignoring her wildly flailing arms and legs.

"If you two are going to fight like that in public," Jack laughed, "you ought to marry her, Morgan."

Morgan had swung her over his shoulder, her shrill cry of protest falling on deaf ears as his long legs began striding from the arena.

"I intend to!" he shot back gruffly, amid the mocking applause and cheers from the audience.

It took a full second for Patty to realize what he had said. Even then she couldn't believe she had heard him correctly or that he had actually meant it. But a spark of hope flickered as her punishing fists stopped hammering his back.

"Morgan —" Her temper dissipated almost as rapidly as it had ignited.

"Shut up!"

He was carrying her through a door into some small office off the arena. As he kicked the door shut with his boot, he swung her to the floor, the momentum nearly carrying her into the wooden desk. Her anger might have receded, but his hadn't in the least. The blue flame of it was blazing hotly in his eyes.

"Whose harebrained idea was that stunt?" Morgan demanded before Patty had a chance to open her mouth.

Her eyes were searching his face, desperately seeking some indication that his previous declaration might have had some foundation in something other than anger or sarcastic mockery.

"What did you say?" Patty asked, holding her breath for his answer.

"I said, whose harebrained idea was that?" he demanded again through tightly clenched teeth, the muscle in his jaw working overtime.

"Jack's," she answered his question absently. "I meant before that. What did you say before that?"

There was a brief flicker of something in his eyes before his look again hardened into an uncompromising mask that told her nothing.

"When?" was his clipped and noncommittal response, impatiently issued.

"Jack said you should marry me and you said you intended to. Or — at least, I — I thought that was what you said," Patty ended lamely.

Her fleeting hope accompanied the downward descent of her heart as the harshness of his expression stayed the same, perhaps growing a little grimmer.

"That's what I said." His mouth thinned into a hard, taut line.

"But you didn't mean it, did you?" she sighed brokenly, a tight catch in her throat that bordered on a sob of despair.

"Yes, I meant it." Morgan growled out the admission. "Somebody's got to keep an eye on you, so you might as well get it through your thick skull right now that it's going to be me!"

There was a broken gasp of delight before Patty threw herself into his arms, circling his waist with her own arms and clinging to him tightly. For an instant, his body was rigid against hers, then it relaxed.

"Hold me, Morgan," her throbbing voice begged, uncaring of how much she was revealing. "Don't ever let me go."

Gently his fingers touched her cheek, then curled beneath her chin to lift her face firmly away from the open collar of his shirt. There was no holding back as Patty gazed into his powerful features, all the love in her heart shining in her brown eyes as she returned his look of wary disbelief with understanding.

"I love you, Morgan," she said simply.

A tiny frown of doubt drew his dark brows together. Then it smoothed away and he bent his head to touch her lips, tenderly at first as though expecting her resistance, then with hungry possession at the unchecked response of hers. She was crushed against him with almost punishing fierceness, but Patty didn't care. The blood roaring in her

216

ears was a wild song of supreme joy.

All too soon Morgan was dragging his mouth from hers, burying it in her chestnut hair as he cradled her tightly against his chest. Patty smiled contentedly into his shirt at the slight tremor that shuddered through him.

"You'd better not be playing some game with me," he warned her thickly, "because I mean to marry you."

"It isn't a game," she promised. "I would be proud to be your wife."

He cupped her face in his hands and examined every detail. "You do love me?" Morgan questioned again. "I can't share you with Lije's ghost."

"You were right all along — it was only a girlhood infatuation," Patty assured him tenderly. "What I felt for Lije is nothing compared to the love I have for you. Lije hasn't meant anything to me as other than a friend for a very long time."

He frowned, "But you kept —"

"No, darling," she laughed easily, "you kept bringing him up. Every time I tried to tell you he didn't matter any more, you kept insisting I was lying."

Groaning at his own stupidity, Morgan kissed his apology. It took a long time to atone fully for his error and Patty enjoyed every minute of it. Finally she was sighing weakly against his chest, drugged by the ardent mastery of his caresses.

"How much time have we wasted?" he murmured against her forehead. "How long have you known?"

"I don't know. Maybe a long time," she whispered with a throbbing ache. "I admitted it to myself at the ranch, but I never dreamed that you might care."

"I should have stayed, shouldn't I?" He smiled wryly. "I thought you were beginning to respond to me. I tried to prod you into admitting it, but you went all cold and prickly again and I gave up."

"I thought you were making fun of me. You were always ordering me around like a child, treating me like a nuisance," Patty murmured, snuggling closer against his chest, needing the reassurance of his uneven heartbeat.

"You were a nuisance," he admitted openly, "to my peace of mind."

"Why were you quitting? Why were you so determined never to see me again?"

She shivered at the pain she had felt at his supposed leaving.

"Surely it's obvious. We were always fighting." The look in his eyes revealed for the first time how their harsh exchanges had hurt him as much as they had hurt her. "I decided that there was no hope. I was certain you despised me. I thought the only thing that was left for me to do was take the advice I'd given you when I told you that as far as you were concerned Lije was dead."

"We were so cruel to each other."

"It's over now," Morgan promised.

He kissed her gently on the corner of her mouth, drawing the response he had anticipated as she turned to seek the warm possession of his kiss.

"You haven't told me you loved me," Patty murmured against his mouth.

Morgan chuckled softly. "I've loved you from the beginning, from almost the first day I saw you over four years ago." The amusement left his voice and a distant pain echoed in his words. "I watched you tagging along after Lije, telling myself one day you would wake up. For nearly three years, you kept it up and I knew I couldn't endure the agony forever. I persuaded my family to sell the rodeo stock. Then Lije got married and I thought I had a chance again." There was a suggestion of a smile in the grooves near his mouth. "Your grandfather knew how much I loved you even then. I'm afraid we did some plotting against you. But you seemed determined not to forget Lije. I

219

tried every way I knew to make you forget. Until this moment, I thought I'd wound up making you hate me."

"I love you," Patty vowed fervently. "I'll never stop loving you."

"I love you. And you'd better not stop loving me, Skinny." The love in his eyes took away the mock threat in his low voice.

"Say that again," she whispered.

"What?" Morgan frowned curiously. "That I love you? I do love you."

"No, Skinny," she answered. "Just now it sounded very much like darling."

"Skinny," he repeated softly, and bent his head as her eyes began to close.

√

THORNDIKE PRESS HOPES you have enjoyed this Large Print book. All our Large Print titles are designed for the easiest reading, and all our books are made to last. Other Thorndike Press Large Print books are available at your library, through selected bookstores, or directly from the publisher. For more information about current and upcoming titles, please call us, toll free, at 1-800-223-6121, or mail your name and address to:

THORNDIKE PRESS
P. O. BOX 159
THORNDIKE, MAINE 04986

There is no obligation, of course.